Dawn Breaks

RAYMOND HAN

Little Rocket Books

Website: www.raymondhan.net
E-mail: han.raymond@hotmail.com

Little Rocket Books, Singapore
ISBN: 978-981-11-5390-7 (pbk.)

**National Library Board, Singapore Cataloguing in
Publication Data**
Name(s): Han, Raymond, 1958-
Title: Dawn breaks / Raymond Han.
Description: Singapore : Little Rocket Books, 2017.
Identifier(s): OCN 1006430337 | ISBN 978-981-11-5390-
7 (paperback)
Subject(s): LCSH: Human cloning--Fiction. | Kidnapping-
-Fiction. | Hostages--Fiction.
Classification: DDC S823--dc23

IN MEMORIAM

In memory of my parents

"Keep moving forward."

Robert J. O'Neill
U.S. Navy SEAL

ALSO BY RAYMOND HAN

THE SUN GAWKS

WHERE THE WIND BLOWS

THE GOLDELL PRISM

SPICE OF LIFE:
SINGAPORE SHORT STORIES

ESSENTIAL GUIDE TO O-LEVEL ENGLISH
COMPOSITION

"An eye for eye only ends up making the whole world blind."

Mahatma Gandhi

ACKNOWLEDGMENTS

My wife, Cindy, has been a steady source of
inspiration in my novel forays.

VISIT THE AUTHOR'S WEBSITE

Find out more about Raymond Han on his
Website
at www.raymondhan.net

CHAPTER 1

It was the clang of metal that woke Kuan Hee. He opened his eyes and took in his surroundings. He found himself in a small room, lying on a thin shabby mattress laid next to a louvred window. Except for this spongy spread, the room was bare. Even the floor was bare screed. A battered wooden door stood about two metres across from him. Sunlight filtering through the shutters above him told him it was day outside. The air was musty; he detected a stench of rotting fish wafting in through the window. He had to be near a wet market or some big rubbish bin. There was a cacophony of noises on the other side of the wall he was now leaning against. It was difficult to make out the voices from the noise.

It had to be early morning, for the wall behind him felt cold against his back. His nose itched, but he could not scratch it. His hands were tied behind his back. He felt pricky fibres poking his wrists. He could only wriggle his legs. They had been bound with a rope. He took a deep breath and sighed heavily. He couldn't open his mouth; it had been taped shut. Soon he got used to the bad odour in the room; he took no notice of it anymore.

Where am I? This is definitely not an HDB flat, Kuan Hee

murmured under his breath. He tried hard to recall what had happened. His mind was still hazy. *Have I been fed with some stupefying drug? What mindless creeps have done this to me? Don't they know it's a capital offence kidnapping someone in Singapore?*

He looked down at his pants. His pockets were not bulging—his iPhone and wallet had been taken from him. There was no way for him to get help. Then he remembered Little Busy was with him. *Where is it now?* The happenings of the recent past slowly drifted into his consciousness.

He had left for work at the university. It was a rainy day and traffic was heavy on the road outside the university. He recalled getting out of his car in the car park. All of a sudden, someone had grabbed him from behind and...

The door creaked open and two men entered the room. One knelt beside Kuan Hee and pressed a moist cloth over his face.

Try as he might to hold his breath, Kuan Hee couldn't stop the involuntary muscles in his body from doing its work. He gasped and took in air. The chloroform finally had its chance to work its magic. He struggled to keep awake. "Lina. Lina," he yelled, but only muffled sounds were heard. He succumbed to the drug and slumped onto his captor's knee. "Lina, where—"

CHAPTER 2

It was as if Lina had heard Kuan Hee's desperate call for help. Or perhaps, it was a loved one's sixth sense. Lina felt a tingling sensation grip her, jolting her thoughts. Something had happened to Kuan Hee. She could feel it in her bones. It wasn't Huei Huei. Huei Huei was in front of her, watching her favourite cartoon on the iPad in their house at 79 Jalan Nuang. She reached for her Samsung smartphone and dialed his number. There was no reply. She tried again several times in vain. Kuan Hee should have reached his office at the Cyborg Intelligence Unit of Temasek University. She called up the reception desk. Kuan Hee had not reported for work today. It was unusual for him to skive. Like his father, Professor Wang, he was a stickler for schedule. And he was also in his element at work. He enjoyed his work in nanotechnology so much that he would forget everything else. Many times, Lina would complain that he had neglected her and Huei Huei. This time, he wasn't in his laboratory. He had no other work place. Kuan Hee also wasn't a social creature. He didn't like to make conversation. Save for Tim and Navin who were his *kakis*, he had a handful of friends. Lina called up every one of them. None could tell her where he was.

Just then the doorbell rang. Lina opened the door to let Xaden in. Eighteen-year-old Xaden was Lina's nephew. It was the school holidays and he had volunteered to fetch lunch for his aunt.

"Aunt Lina. You look flustered."

"I can't get hold of your uncle. I'm afraid something has happened to him."

She took the tiffin carrier from Xaden and spooned out Huei Huei's lunch. With Huei Huei happily enjoying her food and watching YouTube on the iPad, Lina could resume her search for Kuan Hee.

Ignoring Xaden, she sat on the sofa in the living room, hands clasped over her knees, and eyes closed. She took a deep breath. She had to think clearly and not let her muddled thoughts affect her.

"That's it. Why didn't I think of it?"

"What? What is it, Aunt Lina?"

"Little Busy. Your uncle has Little Busy with him. I forgot about it. Now where's the remote?" Little Busy was a metallic robot housefly drone.

Xaden helped her to look for Little Busy's remote control card. They searched the whole house but nothing turned up.

"Look after Huei Huei. I'll go down to the cellar. It should be there."

Lina walked into the study and retrieved a ladder from a hidden corner. She placed it against a floor-to-ceiling bookcase on one wall and climbed it. She tapped on an end panel, which slid open to reveal a small knob. She turned the knob and at once the bookcase rumbled to one side. There was an opening on the wall wide enough for two people to enter. The interior was stark dark. She turned on some switches and light flooded the cellar. She walked down the steps into the secret room, which Kuan Hee's father, Professor Wang, had constructed to hold his inventions. The air was stuffy and warm. The room was slightly smaller than the living room. It held some cupboards, two standing fans and chairs. A large table took centrestage.

Lina opened one of the cupboards and AleXander the two metallic robots glistened in the light. She ignored them and bent down to look at the lower shelf of the cupboard. She spotted two remote control cards. One was Little Busy's and the other Tizzy's. Tizzy was a metallic robot dragonfly drone. She pocketed the two cards.

"Tizzy must be somewhere here too." She opened the small boxes on the shelf. In one, she found the robot dragonfly. She placed it in her other dress pocket and grabbed AleXander the robots.

She paused for a moment, asking herself what else she needed from the cellar. Satisfied she had had everything, she climbed up the steps and returned the bookcase to its original position.

"Aunt Lina, why have you brought out Alex and Xander?"

"In case I need their help. I have a funny feeling we'll soon be falling into adventure again."

"What? Can I join in?"

"Don't interrupt my thoughts. I need to think."

CHAPTER 3

Kuan Hee jolted awake. He opened his eyes. He was feeling drowsy so he saw only floating images. He blinked several times and squinted at his surroundings. He seemed to be in the back of a van. There were windows at the back and on the sides but these were heavily shaded. The vehicle rocked back and forth as if it was in the middle of the ocean. But there wasn't the familiar smell of sea air. And this wasn't a Hippo—one of those amphibious crafts; it was plainly a small van he was in so he was definitely on the road somewhere. But what road in Singapore was as rocky as the one the van was moving on? Kuan Hee searched his memories but could not recall any. *Perhaps, I am on Pulau Ubin.*

Kuan Hee flitted in and out of consciousness. As the drug wore off, he gathered his thoughts. His body was sore all over. He had to have been tied up for many hours. Parts of his arms were numb from resting too long on the floor of the van. He wriggled left and right. He began counting numbers in his mind. He had to keep alert. He couldn't doze off again. He had to be on the lookout for landmarks, if at all he could make out any in these darkened surroundings. He could not see the driver's section. The window separating the two parts of the van had been blocked with an opaque plastic film.

Then the rocking stopped. The van had not stopped moving, but the ride was smooth now. *We are no longer on a kampong track.* Kuan Hee estimated the journey thus far had taken at least three hours. *What journey in Singapore would take so long? Am I in Malaysia? Have they smuggled me across the causeway? Why? How did they do it? How did they manage to get past the eagle-eyed custom officers at the Singapore checkpoint? For sure, these guys couldn't be bribed.* There were so many questions in Kuan Hee's mind but he had no answer for every one of them.

Strangely, his stomach was not grumbling. Was it the sedative effect of the drug? Kuan Hee swallowed his saliva. He had not had a drop of water in ages. *What day is it?* Then the van jerked to a stop. He could hear some people talking outside the van. It was minutes before the door opened and someone jumped into the van. With his eyes shut, Kuan Hee feigned unconsciousness. Through the tiny slit between his eyelashes, he could make out a burly Chinese man with close-cropped hair. He wasn't the same one who came into the room to take him away. Even with his hands free, he was no match for these men, and what's more, his hands and legs were bound. He decided to continue his act.

Kuan Hee allowed the men to heave his limp body onto a metal trolley. They wheeled him along a concrete pavement. Soon this forked into a wooden platform. He could hear the men's boots stomping on the timber floor, which reverberated in sync. *Golly, it's hollow underneath. Am I on a wooden bridge?*

The pungent smell of vaporizing diesel in the air overwhelmed Kuan Hee's senses momentarily. Then the breeze brought a strong musty odour. It conjured up memories of fishing trips with his *kakis*, Tim and Navin, at Changi Point. He had to be close to the sea, but the smell of seawater was absent in the air.

Kuan Hee squinted his eyes. He saw a huge expanse of water in front of him. *Am I near the sea?* There was a long stretch of undulating land in the distance beyond the water. He was not familiar with Malaysian shores and islands but he surmised the land ahead could be an island off the Malaysian coast.

His captors bundled him into a boat, which resembled a small ferry. The boat chugged towards the island.

At last, one of the men spoke. It was a smattering of Mandarin, not of Malaysian-accent variety. Certainly, it wasn't Taiwanese Mandarin. It was Mainland Mandarin he was speaking. He mentioned something about buying *hé fàn*. In Taiwanese Mandarin, boxed meals were *biàndang*.

From the men who delivered a new fridge to his house to the hawker assistants at the neighbourhood coffee shops, Kuan Hee had heard Mainland Mandarin enough times to be able to identify the accent unmistakably. *Why are the Mainland Chinese interested in me?*

Kuan Hee allowed his thoughts to wander. Why had he been kidnapped? He was not rich or influential. Then he remembered Colonel Tee, the late dictator of Singapore. Was it the remnants of his men exacting revenge on their master's behalf? It couldn't be his dad they were after. His dad was safe and sound halfway around the world—in Fort Bragg in North Carolina, the headquarters of the US Special Forces. Professor Wang was doing secretive work in nanotechnology for the United States government.

Then it dawned on him. *They must want something from Dad.* His father was privy to sensitive US state secrets. Just what did they want? Three years ago, he had blasted to smithereens the disks holding the memories of Colonel Tee, so the Colonel could not resurrect himself even if his minions desired to help him do so.

First he had to find out where he was and where he was being taken. It would soon be dark and it would be difficult to make out any landmarks. These Mainland Chinese had the audacity to haul him into the boat in clear view of any passers-by who might be around. But then he had yet to see any passers-by. It had to be a desolate area, Kuan Hee surmised. How was he going to get help? There was not a single soul around to help him. He was resigned to his fate.

The boat reached shore shortly. It was a wooden jetty that the two men disembarked with Kuan Hee in tow. An acoomplice was waiting on the jetty. Rotund and fair, the middle-aged man was starkly different from the able young men who had kidnapped Kuan Hee. He seemed to be in charge, bellowing instructions and waddling about the jetty.

The taller one heaved Kuan Hee over his shoulder and lumbered off the jetty and up the slope to a meandering concrete pavement with the portly supervisor tailing them. Kuan Hee spied a huge house at the top of the slope. As they approached the house, he could see it was a grand old two-storeyed mansion with a large compound. There were Chinese men milling around in front of the building.

Just then a horrifying thought crossed his mind. He had been shanghaied to China. He had landed in some remote part of China, far away from his beloved Lina. She would never be able to find him this time. How did he get himself into this mess?

CHAPTER 4

Little Busy's remote control held the answer to Lina's pressing question—Kuan Hee's whereabouts. It had a feature that could track the robot housefly's position, no matter where it was in the world. The Polaris satellite—that secret American spy satellite in the sky powered the feature. Professor Wang had access to the satellite, courtesy of the United States government for whom he was working. Lina flipped open Little Busy's remote. There was no beeping dot on the map of Singapore, which occupied the entire screen. She pinched the screen to zoom out of the republic. As the map widened to reveal stretches of the Asian continent and part of the South China Sea, she saw something blink on the Indonesian Archipelago, off peninsular Malaysia. She stretched the screen with her fingers. She blinked several times. She couldn't believe her eyes. The blinking dot was hovering over—Lake Toba! Lake Toba in Northern Sumatra was a tourist attraction. It was an idyllic spot for vacation and—trysts!

"That Kuan Hee! He has the gall to drop everything he's doing to hop over to Lake Toba for sexation!"

"Really?" Xaden passed the crayon he was holding to Huei Huei and crossed the room to where Lina was sitting. He stooped next to her, looking at the map on the screen.

"Yeah, *hor*. Uncle Kuan Hee's on Lake Toba."

"Here I am tending to our little baby, and there he is gallivanting around with some hothead."

That night, Lina turned in early. But she could not sleep a wink. She tossed and turned in bed, conjuring what Kuan Hee was up to. *Why should I care? He's likely having a swimmingly good time with some old flame of his this very moment.* Still, she could not bring herself to accept this truth. All along she had thought she was the only world Kuan Hee knew—until little Huei Huei came along. Now, she had to come to terms with some third party sharing this intimacy.

Just then, Lina's smartphone rang. Tim was on the line.

"So, have you found Kuan Hee?"

"He—He's having a secret tryst with some lover."

"Whaaat?"

"He's enjoying himself with his lover somewhere far away."

"Come on, Lina. Don't speak in crypted lingo."

"I'm not. That's what I just said in plain English. That good friend of yours is having the time of his life with another woman in his lap."

There was a long pause.

"You're joking, Lina. You must be. Kuan Hee's not the type, man. I mean, he's a nerd. Nerds don't go fooling around. Hahaha."

"Don't laugh. It's the goddamned truth."

"*Wah piang!* You must be really mad. Fancy you letting foul language out of your mouth. This is—a first!"

There was another long pause.

"Where did you say Kuan Hee's fooling around at?"

"Lake Toba."

"So far away?"

"Yeah. You can't believe it too?"

"No. Not that. It's just not like Kuan Hee. Besides, he's

not been there before. Why should he go to a faraway place he's never been before to do such a thing? I mean, he can go to somewhere nearby—like Geylang."

"Tim! I hate you." She almost wanted to bang down the phone.

"*Alamak!* Lina. Sorry. I didn't mean that. So sorry."

"You men are the same. Always harbouring the thought of having trysts."

"Lina, not me. Certainly, not Kuan Hee."

"I am furious. He has no respect for me. After what we have been through together, after what I've done for him—"

"Lina, pipe down. For goodness's sake, be sane. Kuan Hee is not a Casanova. Think! Something must have happened to Kuan Hee. He doesn't just take off in the middle of work for some fling. He's not that kind of guy. You and I know it. For God's sake, wake up."

The words made some sense to Lina. They quietened her raucous mind. She no longer let expletive-laden language come out of her mouth. What was boiling rage had now turned to simmering fear.

There was another long pause.

"Tim. Could something bad have happened to him?"

"Hey! Lina, why are you blowing hot and cold over Kuan Hee? He's your man. Don't you trust him at all?"

"Tim, I am worried. Has something happened to Kuan Hee?"

"Let's meet, Lina. I'll get Navin. Tomorrow at 10:00 a.m.?"

"Tim, I—alright, 10:00 a.m. here."

CHAPTER 5

It was with a sense of urgency that Tim and Navin stepped into the living room at 79 Jalan Nuang. Lina's harried demeanor added to the tense atmosphere. Little Huei Huei was sitting at the coffee table, busily halving some toy vegetables with a plastic knife.

"Where's Kuan Hee's car?" Tim asked.

"The WheresMyHonda app pinpoints its location at his workplace in Temasek University," Lina said. "The engine monitor says it's been idle for twenty-six hours."

"That's not good news," Tim said, tapping a finger on his forearm. "What does Little Busy's remote say?"

Lina passed the remote to Tim. It was showing the map of North Sumatra, with a blinking dot hovering over Lake Toba.

"The blinking dot hasn't moved?" Tim asked.

"Been like that since yesterday," Lina said.

"What time did you first know Kuan Hee's in Lake Toba?" Navin asked.

"I don't know. I think. Yes. Yesterday afternoon. Xaden was here, delivering lunch," Lina said.

"And you didn't tell us until late last night?" Navin said.

"Sorry. I couldn't think clearly," Lina said. She was almost in tears. She blamed herself for wasting precious time tending to her doubts.

"Let's put the pieces together, before we decide on a plan of action," Tim said. "Kuan Hee's not at the office. His car is at the university. He's uncontactable. Little Busy's GPS shows it's been in Lake Toba since early yesterday afternoon. The lake is two hours away by air."

"No doubt about it," Navin said. "He's got to be there."

"Yes, looks like it," Tim said. "We need to go there right away—before his captors have a chance to act."

"Time is of the essence," Navin said. "He could…" He stopped short of telling them the dire consequences of their late action; Lina was in no state to hear such things.

"Let me check the next available flight to Medan," Tim said. He took out his iPhone and spent the next few minutes browsing the flight apps.

"There're two flights—1:40 p.m. today and 7:40 a.m. tomorrow," Tim said.

"We can't wait till tomorrow," Lina screeched. "It might be too late!"

"Let's go today, then," Navin said.

"That gives us less than three hours," Tim said.

"Let's do it," Navin said.

"I'll book the tickets. Get your passports—and Kuan Hee's too," Tim said. "How did they get him out of Singapore without a passport? Never mind. We won't have time to purchase rupiah. We'll do it in Medan. Anyway, it's cheaper there."

"I will take Huei Huei over to my mother's place," Lina said. "Shall we meet there?"

"Have we forgotten anything?" Tim said.

"How are we going to the airport?" Navin asked.

"I'll uber a ride for us," Tim said.

"I'll bring along the robots and Tizzy too," Lina said.

"Don't forget to book hotel rooms," Navin said.

"No need," Tim said. "I'll call my uncle afterwards. We'll stay with him. He lives in Medan."

"You have a relative there?" Navin said. "You never said anything about having relatives overseas."

"You know I'm not a blabbermouth," Tim said. "Let's get going."

CHAPTER 6

As Flight MI234 descended over Medan in Indonesia, it gave its occupants a sweeping close-up view of the low-lying mishmash of residential districts encircling Polonia Airport.

Polonia Airport was a world away from Changi Airport. Stepping into the airport was akin to stepping back into Singapore of the early 1980s. While Singapore's Changi Airport had improved by bounds and leaps, Medan's Polonia Airport had stagnated. You could say Polonia Airport was only a provincial airport, but the stark difference between the two airports was revealing of faultlines in management.

Flight MI234 taxied to a stop outside the terminal. Tim, Navin and Lina stepped out of the aircraft onto a boarding staircase. Together with the other passengers, they climbed down the flight of steps and packed into a coach, which unloaded them at the arrival section of the terminal building.

Tim kept an eye out for his uncle and cousin. They were supposed to meet him at the airport today. It was difficult to make them out in a sea of faces. Polonia Airport was humming with passengers and visitors today.

The customs officer attending to the trio removed a carton of cigarettes from several that Tim had brought into the country for his uncle. Tim protested in vain. Perhaps, it was this that led to the trio being detained at the arrival terminal. A customs officer said Tim had come too often to Medan. He took the three friends to a small room in a corner of the arrival hall.

Half an hour later, he released them. They found themselves standing in front of Tim's uncle and his cousin. The three friends exchanged greetings with Uncle Kenny and Harry. Uncle Kenny was middle-aged and balding. He was Tim's mother's elder brother. Harry was Uncle Kenny's only son. He was a twentysomething tanned and handsome lad. He had his father's high forehead. He was also almost as tall as Tim.

"Uncle Kenny, the guy at the counter confiscated a carton of Marlboro I brought in for you," Tim said.

"It's OK," Uncle Kenny said. "Don't let it bother you too much."

"The immigration chap also said I had come here too often. I told him I visited you once every few months but he was adamant that I had an ulterior motive for coming here so he detained us," Tim said.

"He just wants coffee money," Uncle Kenny said.

"Did you give him any?" Tim asked.

"One million rupiahs," his uncle said.

"What? That's corruption," Tim said.

"It's a way of life here, Tim," his uncle said. "We are used to it. Anyway, it's just peanuts. Don't let it bother you."

"Uncle Kenny, such things don't happen in Singapore," Navin said.

"Of course. That's why Medan is so underdeveloped," Uncle Kenny said. "The good thing is—we can get things moving fast this way."

"Luckily, they didn't query us about AleXander the robots," Tim said.

"Robots? What robots?" Harry asked.

"Erh. It's a long story, Harry. I'll tell you later," Tim said.

"Uncle Kenny, thanks for putting us up," Lina said. She wanted to put a stop to the conversation about the two robots; they were within earshot of everyone in the arrival hall of the airport.

"It's our pleasure," Uncle Kenny said. "I'm sorry to hear about your husband. We'll find him if he is in Lake Toba. Harry will be your guide in town. You'll all be in good hands with him around."

"Yes, I know North Sumatra like the back of my hands," Harry said.

"Thanks," the three friends chorused in unison.

Everyone packed into a Toyota Camry which cruised through rickety neighbourhoods till it came to a stop on the side of a small road—more like a lane—straddling rows of tightly packed concrete shophouses, some of which were shorter than the others, but all of which were no taller than four storeys.

"Harry, why don't you have auto-pilot for the Camry?" Navin asked.

"Such technology has yet to trickle down to us here," Harry said. "Perhaps, in ten years, if we are lucky."

"You must be joking," Navin said.

"Navin, Indonesia is a big country, unlike Singapore," Tim said. "There are over one hundred million people. It's not an easy job managing such a big population."

"Besides," Harry said. "We don't need the latest technology. It's not really useful here because we don't have the infrastructure to support high-tech stuff." He pointed at the road ahead. "My house is just in front—on the left."

228A Jalan Muara Takus was a three-storeyed shophouse unit but unlike other units along the row, its first storey was vacant. It was the Camry's garage. The Chen family lived on the upper floors of this unit. Next door to this unit was Toko Harry, a modern provision shop housed in a double-unit shophouse. The shop, run by Harry, catered both to the neighbourhood and the expatriate community.

"*Wah!* Tim, your uncle must be rich," Navin said. "He owns three units here."

"He doesn't just own the units here," Tim said. "He has other properties in Medan. He has businesses catering to the American expatriate community for which he gets paid in hard United States currency, not rupiah."

"Come, let me show you your rooms," Harry said. He led the visitors up a narrow concrete staircase located on one side of the shophouse. The third storey was where Uncle Kenny and Harry lived. The second storey had two rooms—both vacant. Lina was to occupy one and the two men the other.

"My father's gone to the restaurant. He wants to check for himself things are in shipshape order," Harry said. "Make yourselves at home." He excused himself and disappeared downstairs.

Lina was in a hurry. She wanted to throw her things down and get down to searching for Kuan Hee at once, but it was not possible. This was Medan, a city of three million people. It was strange territory for the three friends. They were helpless without Harry and he needed time to make arrangements for their trip to Lake Toba.

Noticing her impatience, Tim said, "Lina, we are in a foreign land. This is no walk in the park."

"Kuan Hee is still in Lake Toba. The blinking dot hasn't moved," Lina said. "I haven't let my eyes off the screen since we left the Polonia Airport."

"Don't fret, Lina," Navin said. "We'll find Kuan Hee, if it's the last thing we do. We're best friends right?"

Lina allowed a smile to peep out of her face. But it quickly deflated with Tim's next remark.

"Harry says we can only set out early next morning," Tim said. "He can only lay his hands on a van tonight."

"We can set off tonight then," Lina said.

"Lina, this is not Singapore," Tim said, "where the street lights go on at a flick of a switch and everywhere is in brightness. Here, most of the roads do not have any streetlights. And many of them have potholes. It's too dangerous to travel in the dark."

"Yeah. Tim is right," Navin said. "Let's wait for Harry to get back."

That evening, Harry returned with—not a van—but a minibus he had borrowed from a friend. It had ample space for all of them and Kuan Hee too when they rescued him. Harry was busy washing the minibus on the side of the road when Navin popped downstairs.

"Can I lend you a hand?" Navin said.

"No need," Harry said. "Almost finished. Had your dinner?"

"Yes," Navin said.

As the water splashed onto the sidewalk and into the drain, Navin could see the water in the drain glistening under the streetlight. Curious, he stooped to take a closer look.

"It's mosquitoes," Harry said. "Mosquito larvae and pupae."

"*Ha*?" Navin said. "But the whole drain is glistening."

"Yes, they are all over the drain," Harry said. "But nobody bothers here. You don't get fined here."

With the cleaning done, Harry knelt down by the drain and motioned for Navin to join him.

"Here, we have our little conversations while squatting along the sidewalk," Harry said. "It's our way of life."

"Oh, really?" Navin said. "Well, as the saying goes, when in Rome do as Romans do." He squatted next to Harry who offered him a cigarette.

"No thanks," Navin said. "I don't smoke. We don't smoke."

Harry took a long puff and expelled the clove-flavoured smoke away from Navin but some of it wafted into Navin's nose. "Where's your missus?" He asked.

"Gosh! I'm not married yet," Navin said.

"Why do Singapore men marry late?" Harry asked. "Tim is also unattached. I've asked him several times, and each time he tells me he hasn't met the right girl."

"You ask so much about us. You must be married right?" Navin said. "But I don't see your wife."

"She's visiting her parents in Jakarta," Harry said. "She'll be back in two weeks."

"When did you get married?" Navin asked.

"Five years ago," Harry said. "My daughter is already four years old."

"You have a four-year-old daughter?" said Navin in disbelief. "Indonesian men do marry young."

"Our girls marry even younger," Harry said. "If they are not married by the time they are twenty-three, they will be left on the shelf forever."

"S-e-r-i-o-u-s?" Navin said.

"It's the truth," Harry said. "You still haven't told me why you are still single."

"Actually, I will be getting married next year," Navin said.

"That's great news. What is your girlfriend working as?" Harry said.

"I don't know," Navin said. "I haven't met her yet." "Really?" Harry exclaimed. "How come you're marrying someone you haven't even seen?"

"It's our custom," Navin said. "My mother arranged this marriage for me. The girl lives in Hyderabad in South India. She's working for my mother's cousin who runs a business dealing in pearls."

There was a moment of silence while Harry digested the explanation.

"I wouldn't marry someone I don't love," Harry said, let alone someone I haven't even met."

"As I have said," Navin explained curtly, "it's our

21

Indian custom. It's been like this for a thousand years."

"Is she a child bride?" Harry asked.

"*Alamak!* Nothing like it," Navin said. "She will be twenty-one this December."

"I see," Harry said.

"Actually, we Chinese also had arranged marriages in the past," Tim said. He had just come outside and saw it fit to wade into the conversation to save the situation. "In fact, for thousands of years, it's been like that. Even now, it's happening in some places."

"What's that you were saying about robots?" Harry asked. He had suddenly remembered Tim's remark at the airport.

Tim was glad the conversation had taken a turn. He regaled Harry with an account of the adventures of Alex and Xander the robots.

"Wow! I thought such things only happened in comics and movies," Harry said. "Can they really do the things you just said? Can I see them in action?"

"Come on up to our room," Tim said. "We'll show you. I mean—we'll let Lina show you. She's their master."

"You mean, half their master," Navin said.

"Oh yeah, Kuan Hee's the real owner," Tim said.

Soon Harry was enjoying the antics of the two robots in the company of the three visitors.

"This is their latest feat," Lina said. "Alex and Xander can climb walls." She uttered an order to the two robots. At once, they ran up the wall of the room. Then they were dangling from the ceiling.

"Wow! How do they do it?" Tim asked. "They are defying gravity."

"Kuan Hee's father has fitted their feet with millions of special microscopic hair," Lina said.

"Hair can stick on the wall?" Harry asked in disbelief.

"You mean the same type of hair found on lizards' toes?" Navin said.

"Not really," Lina said. "But the properties are similar."

"Spectacular. Simply spectacular," Harry said.

"Yeah. I agree," Navin said.

"One question, Lina," Harry said. "Can they fly?"

"Hey Harry, that's asking too much of them," Tim said.

"I've asked Kuan Hee this question. He says it's still in science fiction realm," Lina said.

"What's that?" Harry asked.

"Lina means it may be possible in the near future," Navin said. "It is not impossible."

"I see," Harry said.

"Have you got the hardware I was asking you for?" Tim said.

"Er. Yes," Harry said. He got up from the floor and excused himself from the room.

"What hardware?" Lina asked.

"I didn't tell you guys earlier," Tim said. "I asked for some weapons."

"Aren't Alex and Xander enough?" Lina said. "They are pretty powerful, you know."

"We don't know who or what we are dealing with," Tim said. "We need to be well-prepared. We can't afford to fail. Kuan Hee's life is at stake."

"Is it easy to get guns here?" Navin asked.

"Nope, not guns. Rifles," Tim said. "It's easy to get these here. Money talks."

Harry returned hauling a longish bag. He fished out three Steyr AUGs and handed them to the three friends.

"Three enough?" Harry asked.

Tim took the olive green Steyr AUG in his hands and examined it carefully. Then he pulled the charging handle. It snapped into place. He pressed the rifle stock against his shoulder and grapped its fore grip. "An A3 M1. Compact. Short barrel. The charging handle is not obtrusive, unlike the original AUG. Allows one-handed shooting just in case. Love the pistol grip. Pretty old, but will do the job. I like it."

"It's light and fits into a backpack easily," Navin said.

"How do I use this contraption?" Lina asked.

"It's not for you," Tim said. "You just sit around and look pretty." Lina at once contorted her face. *Tim always annoys me.*

Harry poured out six loaded magazines onto the floor.

"Each magazine holds ten rounds," Harry said.

"Should be enough," Tim said.

"You can get assault rifles here?" Navin asked.

"We need some protection in the city," Harry said. "Just in case of unrest."

"Unrest?" Lina said. "What type of unrest?"

"Civil unrest," Harry said. "It happens once in a long while. People attack businesses and loot shops."

"*Wah!* That's serious," Navin said.

"Happened here?" Lina asked.

"Yes, in Medan not too long ago. Thousands of students and local residents swooped down onto the neighbourhood. They threw stones and looted shops," Harry said.

"So the government allows you to buy such weapons?" Navin said.

"No," Harry said. "We get them through illegal channels. These are a must-have. We hide them away."

"What if they do a spot check?" Navin asked.

"They will never find the weapons," Harry said. "Besides, money settles everything."

"What caused the unrest?" Lina asked.

"Steep price rises," Harry said. "Such things are out of our control, but people blame us businesses."

"But it looks so peaceful outside," Lina said.

"Looks can be deceiving," Harry said.

"How far away from Medan is Lake Toba?" Navin asked.

"One hundred and eighty five kilometres," Harry said. "It will take half a day to travel there by road."

"So, when are we leaving for Lake Toba?" Lina asked.

"At dawn," Tim said. "We'd better get some sleep. It's

going to be a long day tomorrow."

CHAPTER 7

"Finally!" Lina exclaimed as the minibus pulled off from the side of the road and drove past the rows of shophouses that lined Jalan Muara Takus. It was dawn and the neighbourhood was still asleep. As the minibus reached the junction, Harry slowed down to allow two men time to pull aside a wooden barricade to let them through. He waved to them and they waved back. The minibus drove into Jl. Kh. Zainul Arifin, a thoroughfare in Medan.

"Why is the street barricaded?" asked Navin.

"To keep unsavoury elements away from the neighbourhood," Tim said. He was in the front seat with Harry.

"Yeah, we pay these thugs to protect us," Harry said.

"These are gangsters?" said Lina. Harry nodded.

"Harry. Is your mother out of town?" Lina asked.

There was a long silence in the driver's section of the minibus.

"Our mothers died in an air crash years ago," Tim said. "We were toddlers then."

An uneasy silence fell in the minibus.

"I'm terriby sorry," Lina said. "Kuan Hee didn't tell

26

me. I didn't know."

"It's alright," Tim said. "Happened so long ago."

"How did it happen?" Navin asked.

"They were returning to Medan from Jakarta. There was bad weather and visibility was poor. The plane crashed into the woodlands near Polonia Airport," Harry said. "I was too young then. I can't recollect the happenings, but I daren't ask my father. I don't want him to be sad."

"Your father didn't remarry?" Lina asked.

"Lina!" Navin interrupted.

"Lina, you just don't know when to shut your gap," Tim said.

"Oh sorry," Lina said. "I didn't think."

"It's alright, Lina," Harry said. "Honest, I'm fine."

"Just don't bring it up again," Tim said.

Silence returned to the minibus for the next few minutes.

"Don't say a word," Harry said. "Let me handle the police, if they turn up."

"Aye. Aye. Captain," Navin said. Lina broke into laughter. The uneasy silence that reigned moments ago was soon forgotten. In its place was animated chatter. Everyone was excited about the mission.

"We'll stop over in Brastagi. I need to pick up a friend. He knows Lake Toba well. He has contacts there," Harry said.

About two hours into their journey southwards, the three friends realized they were heading into the highlands. The roads were cobbled and the ride was bumpy. Lina opened a window and poked her face out to take in the fresh morning air. At once, cold air descended on her face, caressing it.

"It must be below sixteen degrees Centigrade outside," Lina said. "My face feels like it's been in a freezer."

"Brastagi is 1,300 metres above sea level," Harry said.

"*Wah seh*, that's really tall," Lina said. "Bukit Timah Hill is only one hundred plus metres."

"Lina, Bukit Timah Hill isn't a hill—more like a slope," Navin said.

Ahead of the minibus, a tanned handsome lad with a shock of messy hair and an impish grin waved. He looked like he had yet to do national service. Harry stopped the vehicle by the side of the road. Everyone got down for a breather. They had been crammed into the vehicle for too long and needed to stretch their legs.

The air in Brastagi was indeed cold. It had the three friends wishing Singapore weather could be like this every day. Not freezing cold—that would be too uncomfortable, but cold enough to enjoy the day without reaching for some tissue paper to absorb the sweat. The three friends rubbed their hands as they surveyed the surroundings. Except for a lone ramshackle shack, it was all undulating greenery around them and some peaks—great places to watch sunrise. The road was no more than sandy track beatened by years of use.

Harry was busy chatting with his friend in Bahasa Indonesia. They seemed to be catching up with each other. Then he brought the others into the conversation. Alfredo was a Batak. He had lived in the highlands all his life. He listened intently and nodded as Harry introduced his three friends from Singapore. But he really didn't understand English. All he knew was a smattering of English words such as 'thank you', 'good' and 'goodbye', phrases he had picked up over the years from acquaintances.

"Alfredo knows Lake Toba like the back of his hands," Harry said. "We'll be safe in his hands."

"How come he's got a Christian name?" Navin asked.

"He's a Christian," Harry said.

"I thought Indonesians are Muslims," Lina said.

"He's a Batak Karo—they're mostly Christians," Harry said.

Just then, Alfredo waved to someone passing by on a motorized pushcart. The vendor stopped his makeshift stall and placed skewered ears of corn atop a charcoal-fired grill. Minutes later, he handed the sticks of toasted, lightly blackened corn to the visitors.

The corn was deliciously sweet. "These have been buttered," Harry explained. "It's a local favourite. Cheap and nourishing."

The three friends were glad for the treat. They hadn't had a bite all morning and were ravenous. They devoured almost an entire basket of corn on the cart.

"Tim, you ride in the back," Harry said. "Alfredo will take the front with me. He will guide me all the way to Parapat."

"Where's Parapat? Is that our next stop?" Lina asked.

"Parapat is the gateway to Lake Toba," Harry said. "We take a boat to Lake Toba from there. By the way, Lake Toba is known as Danau Toba here. The island on the lake is Samosir Island."

With its occupants' stomachs satiated, the minibus continued its journey along the hilly terrain southwards towards Parapat town.

CHAPTER 8

Magnificent Samosir Island loomed into view across a large expanse of water on the right as the minibus wound its way along a small road hugging the contours of the hilly terrain near the banks of the lake.

Lina shuddered as she peered out of the window. Each time the minibus perilously negotiated a bend on the small road, she shut her eyes. A mere metre of ground stood between the road shoulder and the edge of the cliff. There were no guardrails on the lake's side to guide the driver's eyes. It was a sudden drop from a great height if the minibus careened off the road. Alfredo was at the wheel. A seasoned driver along this part of the country, he effortlessly guided the minibus along the long and winding road towards Parapat.

Lina did not have the mood to take in the spectacular view of the lake or the longish island. She was now near to her beloved who was somewhere on the island. Unfolding Little Busy's remote, she pinched and dragged the screen to enlarge the map of North Sumatra on it. As Samosir Island grew bigger on the screen, roads and places appeared out of nowhere. They dotted the entire island. The blinking dot hovered over a spot near Pondok Wisata

Lagundi Samosir on the west of the island.

"Kuan Hee hasn't moved," Lina said. "He's still near this place Pondok something."

"I still can't figure out why these people brought him here," Tim said. "Doesn't make sense to me."

"We'll find out soon enough," Navin said.

"Alfredo is taking us to a place where we can put down our things and take a rest," Harry said.

"We aren't going to the island right now?" Lina said, disappointed.

"In good time, Lina," Tim said. "Anyway, we're already here, right? Kuan Hee's within sight, right?"

The minibus pulled into Parapat town and cruised through its narrow roads along the banks of the lake. It drove up a slope, past a sign saying Atsari Hotel and stopped in the driveway of a two-storeyed building overlooking the lake.

"This is the place," Harry said. "The jetty's a walk away and we can rent a speedboat at this hotel."

"I like it," Tim said. "It's away from prying eyes of locals and others."

"It looks modern," Navin said. "No more than twenty years old."

The five friends checked into two rooms on the second storey of the hotel. From the rooms, they had a paranomic view of the lake and Samosir Island. Below, the shore was only a stone's throw away. In front of them, idyllic Danau Toba masked the danger the visitors were heading into.

"We need to feed our stomachs first," Tim said, "before we have a powwow." He ordered room service through the phone in the room. "They serve Western food too."

"Why can't we stay in a hotel on the island?" Lina asked. "There are a few spread throughout the island."

"We need a getaway hideout," Tim said. "A safe spot far from the place where these kidnappers are holding Kuan Hee."

Lina nodded. Now she understood. It was for everyone's safety that Tim had made the arrangement to stay in Atsari Hotel instead of on the island. She was secretly glad Kuan Hee and she had levelheaded Tim as their close friend.

It had taken the three friends four days to get this close to Kuan Hee. They had to plan carefully; his safety was in their hands.

Everyone crowded around a twin bed in the men's room. Lina unfolded Little Busy's remote and pointed to Kuan Hee's current location on the map. The screen was too small for everyone to take a good look, so Tim laid down his iPad for Lina to swipe the map from the remote onto the iPad. He enlarged the map of Samosir Island. At once, buildings and roads popped up on the map.

Next Harry explained the local terrain to the group. He told the group that the place Kuan Hee was being held in was a desolate area, off the tourist track.

"Lina, can we get 'live' pictures of Kuan Hee?" Tim asked.

"I'll try," Lina said. She turned on the camera feature on the remote. At once, the iPad screen turned stark black.

"It's been like this all the while," Lina said. "No matter what I do, I cannot get the screen to light up."

"It's not working?" Harry asked.

"Little Busy is in a darkened place—perhaps in Kuan Hee's pocket," Tim said. "Lina, get it to fly around."

With Lina at its controls, Little Busy flitted into action and hovered in the contained space it was in.

"Use its night-vision feature," Tim said. In her anxiety, Lina had forgotten the robot drone could see in the dark. She tapped an icon and at once warm reds and cool blues competed for screen space.

"Little Busy is in some tight spot—like a cabinet," Lina said.

"Looks like a drawer to me," Navin said. "The contours are narrow. Little Busy can only move forward or backward."

"Navin's right," Tim said. "Little Busy's stuck in this place. We have to wait till someone opens the drawer."

"The robot can't drill through the drawer?" said Harry.

"It's not designed for that," Lina said, disappointed. She had been hoping to see Kuan Hee's face.

"Lina, don't fret," Tim said. "Keep trying." Lina nodded.

"We're all behind you, Lina," Navin said.

"Let's discuss our plan of action," Tim said. "First, I would like to say this—it's near impossible to succeed on a first attempt." He paused for a moment as if to catch his breath. Then he continued. "But, we are here to do the impossible—and succeed the first time."

Everyone nodded in unison. Alfredo merely imitated the others. He actually didn't understand a word Tim had said. He was glad Harry was doing the translation for him.

Tim shared his plan for rescuing Kuan Hee. They would go to the island in a speedboat and alight at Pondok Wisata Lagundi Samosir—a jetty on the island. From there, they would make their way on foot. Navin and Lina were to wait in the speedboat at the jetty. Tim, Harry and Alfredo would set off to save Kuan Hee.

Then Tim lugged a big bag onto the bed and fished out the Steyr AUGs. At the same time, Alfredo drew a rifle from the backpack behind him and placed it on the bed.

"M16. May I?" Tim said. He lifted the rifle and made a few snap motions with it. "Solid dependable piece," he declared to his audience.

"What about Alex and Xander?" Lina asked.

"Alex will follow me," Tim said, "and Xander will be with you and Navin. We also need to bring Tizzy along, Lina." Tizzy was a robot dragonfly drone. Both Little Busy and Tizzy were Professor Wang's creations.

"Don't worry," Lina said. "I won't forget."

"When do we move?" Navin asked.

"Tomorrow, at the crack of dawn," Tim said. "Harry,

how about the speedboat?"

"Settled," Harry said. "I'm getting it tonight."

"OK! Let's get down to cleaning the weapons," Tim said.

CHAPTER 9

Lake Toba looked the picture of calm and serenity this morning as the five friends crowded into a speedboat at the jetty. Not a sound pierced the still morning air. Nothing stirred at such an unearthly hour in the idyllic surroundings.

Alfredo proved he was not only a good driver, but also a capable speedboat pilot. He seemed to be a jack-of-all-trades. It was simply handy having him around. He seemed to be at home at the wheel of the speedboat. The speedboat broke the silence of the night as it spurted and hummed its way through the placid waters of the lake, leaving a trail of white as it sped parallel to the island, heading for its destination south of the island.

It was a twenty-minute ride to the jetty on Samosir Island. There was not a soul in sight as the speedboat slowed to a stop at the jetty. The moonlight was the only illumination on the entire stretch of shore.

On the jetty, Navin was careful to conceal his Steyr AUG in his bag. It was cocked and ready for action. Xander stood at Lina's side while she kept her eyes trained on Little Busy's screen—just in case. They could see each other, but anyone farther away from them could only make out their shadows, for it was too dark.

Tim and Harry followed Alfredo along the jetty to a wide walkway hugging the slope of a hill. Visibility was poor so they had to stay close to one another. Alfredo gave the signal for them to get down on their knees. They crouched down in single file and retrieved their rifles from their bags.

A footpath, which wound with the contour of the hill, stood metres above these intruders. It led to a big house perched on top of the hill.

The intruders needed eyes on the hilltop, so it was time for Tizzy to do its work. Tim released the robot dragonfly into the air. It flapped its wings and flew upwards towards the house on top. As it ascended the slope, its cameras gave the intruders a bird's eye view of the elevated grounds. Young trees dotted the slope with small open spaces between them.

As Tizzy flew higher, a large compound appeared on the screen. Wall spotlights lit part of the compound, leaving the other parts in darkness. There was a driveway in it. At one end of the driveway stood a large two-storeyed house with a gabled roof and red brick walls. A wide verandah hugged the perimeter of both floors of the building. In the verandahs, white-painted French windows lined the walls. On the upper floor, a lone Chinese guard sat huddled in a chair. A rifle rested on the balustrade parapet in front of him. The guard had the entire compound in his sights, but he appeared to be dozing.

Tizzy flitted along the verandah on the ground floor, peeping through the glazed French doors as it flew past them.

"We're going nowhere letting Tizzy fly all over the place," Harry said. "It's too big and we don't have time."

"Ah! I forgot I have the coordinates of Little Busy's location," Tim said. He fished out of his pocket a slip of paper Lina had given him. In it, she had written the information.

"Let's compare coordinates," Tim said. He swiped the screen and tapped the set of numbers onto the screen's search box. At once a grid appeared, superimposing a blinking dot onto a map of their immediate surroundings. Now there were two blinking dots. One showed Tizzy's real-time position, the other Little Busy's.

"The dots are very close to each other," Harry said. "Both are in the building."

"Yes, we need more details," Tim said. He enlarged the map so that it zoomed into the big building. He tapped an icon and the infrared scanner in Tizzy threw up a skeleton plan of the entire house on the screen with both dots blinking in different spots.

Tim pointed to the screen. "This blinking dot is where Tizzy is—in the verandah, west of the house. The other dot seems to be in the second last room on the east end. Question is—upper or lower floor?" He tapped on the screen again to bring up a front elevation of the house.

"Wow!" Harry said. "How did you do that?"

"Magic," Tim said as he fingered the blinking dot on the screen. "Ground floor—second last room. Time for Tizzy to get moving again." He manoeuvred Tizzy to the other side of the house.

"How can we be sure Kuan Hee is in the same room as Little Busy?" Harry asked.

"We can't," Tim said. "We can only hope he is."

Tizzy was now hovering outside the room. It swerved downwards to the bottom of the door and crawled through the small opening between the door and the floor. Then it flitted upwards, propelling itself towards the centre of the room.

"There's Kuan Hee!" Tim said. He piloted Tizzy towards a dark figure on a mattress laid on the floor. He switched on Tizzy's spotlights. At once the area in front of the robot dragonfly lit up. Kuan Hee's dishevelled hair shone in the light. In sleep, he looked tired and bedraggled.

"Kuan Hee. Kuan Hee," Tim called out through the

tiny speakers on Tizzy's head. Kuan Hee stirred. Then he opened his eyes and blinked several times. Tizzy's tiny lights had blinded him momentarily. He squinted and allowed his mouth to widen into a weak smile.

"Tim, is that you?" Kuan Hee said. He tried to get up but fell onto the mattress. It was a difficult act as his hands were tied to his back and his legs were bound too.

"Take it easy, old chap," Tim said. Kuan Hee tried again and this time succeeded in raising himself against the wall.

"Lina, where's she?" Kuan Hee asked. "Lina, are you here too?"

"Lina is nearby," Tim said. "She's down at the jetty with Navin. I'm here with my cousin and his friend. We are below the hill now."

"Where am I?" Kuan Hee asked. "Where's this place?"

"Lake Toba," Tim said.

"Lake Toba in Indonesia?" Kuan Hee said. "I'm not in China?"

"No time for small talk now, Kuan Hee," Tim said. "Let's get you out of here first. Hang on! We are coming up the hill now." Tim pocketed the remote and discussed a plan of action with Harry and Alfredo. Then he took out Alex from his backpack. The men cocked their rifles and began climbing the hill with Alex at their heels. They had not seen any other guards through Tizzy's cameras. It was apparent Kuan Hee's captors were not expecting an intrusion. Their guard was down; it was the best time to strike.

From the edge of the compound, the three intruders could make out the Chinese guard on the upper floor. He had yet to wake from his slumber. There was no one in the open area. However, there were two CCTV cameras perched on the pillars of the house. Together, they gave a complete coverage of the compound. Someone could be monitoring the cameras. They had to knock out the camera watching the east side of the house.

The intruders trod as lightly as they could to the corner of the building. Tim pressed a protruding button on the back of the robot and its front panel opened. He whispered some commands. At once, Alex leapt onto the wall and shuffled up to the second level where the CCTV camera was perched. It released a short burst of laser beams, which melted the camera lens. Then it returned to where Tim was standing.

"Let's go do our job," Tim said. The three men stalked through the verandah in single file. Outside the second last room, Harry and Alfredo kept the verandah in their rifles' sights while Tim got down to breaking open the door with Alex's help. In seconds, the robot burned a hole through the lock with its laser. Tim pushed the door open and all three moved swiftly into the room with Alfredo keeping watch at the door.

"Tim!" Kuan Hee whimpered. "Thank goodness you are here."

Tim was all smiles as he unfastened the ropes on Kuan Hee's hands and legs. Kuan Hee wobbled as he struggled to stand. His legs were numb from disuse. Tim and Harry had to help keep him stable on his feet.

"My iPhone…Little Busy…They're in that drawer," Kuan Hee said. He was too weak to reach the drawer. Tim opened the drawer and retrieved the iPhone and a wallet. Before he could grab Little Busy, it flitted into the air, prancing and dancing as if it was delighted to be free at last. In fact, it was Lina at the controls. She had been glued to the remote's screen and was hopping with joy when the screen finally played 'live' images of a limping Kuan Hee.

"Look at the way Little Busy's buzzing through the air. Lina must be elated," Tim said.

"Kuan Hee. Meet my cousin Harry and his friend Alfredo," Tim said. Kuan Hee smiled at the two men.

"We must hurry," Harry said.

The two men slung their rifles and helped Kuan Hee out of the room and through the verandah, with Alfredo and Alex behind them.

"So far so good," Tim muttered under his breath as they scrambled down the slope towards the jetty. It was too good to believe. They had not fired a single shot in their rescue mission. Would luck turn against them now, just when they were relishing success?

Lina and Navin ran towards the three men as they hobbled onto the jetty. Lina flapped around Kuan Hee. She had missed him so much.

"Lina, wait till we put him down," Tim said.

The group hurried to the speedboat with Navin and Alfredo covering their backs. Once everyone was safely in the speedboat, Alfredo shifted the control handle forward and at once the speedboat sliced through the calm waters as it raced towards the mainland.

"Kuan Hee, I missed you so," Lina cried as she hugged Kuan Hee. Tears were welling in her eyes.

"Aw! I can't *tahan* this," Tim said. "It's overwhelming my senses."

"For goodness's sake, stop teasing her, Tim," Navin said.

Kuan Hee blinked. He was relishing his newfound freedom. He squeezed Lina's hand. It was good she was at his side again.

CHAPTER 10

It was almost noon when the six friends gathered in Lina's room. Kuan Hee had regained his strength and could move about unaided.

"It's good to see you guys again," Kuan Hee said.

"Yes, thanks to you all," Lina added.

"How did they get you into Indonesia?" Navin asked.

Kuan Hee shook his head. "I really have no idea. When I woke up, I was already somewhere in Indonesia, I think. I actually thought I was in some part of China."

"Actually, nothing's impossible in Indonesia," Harry said, "with money, of course."

"Is that so?" Navin said.

"It also helps if you have connections," Harry said.

"You mean anyone can be smuggled in and out of the country just like that?" Navin snapped his fingers to make his point.

Harry nodded. "We have a long coastline. It's difficult for the authorities to monitor."

"Then there is another question—how did the kidnappers smuggle you out of Singapore, Kuan Hee?" Kuan Hee shook his head again.

"It's rare that you do not have answers to my

questions," Tim said. "You always have a ready answer for everything."

"They didn't even use his passport," Lina said. "It's with me." She waved his passport for everyone to see.

"It can't be that the kidnappers bought off the immigration officers," Tim said.

"Yeah," Navin said. "For sure, you can't buy off our immigration officers."

"I don't know how I can get home," Kuan Hee said. "I don't think the Indonesian immigration officers will let me leave. There's no arrival *chop* in the passport."

"It's an easy problem to solve, Kuan Hee," Harry said. "I'll get your passport stamped."

"Just like that?" Navin said.

"Yeah. It's that simple," Harry said.

"Thanks, Harry," Tim said. "I owe you one."

"No sweat. We are cousins, Tim," Harry said.

"Thanks for coming to my rescue," Kuan Hee said.

"*Aiyah*," Navin said. "Can we stop all these 'thank you' stuff? We are good friends, aren't we? And good friends help each other. Period."

"Navin's right," Tim said.

Alfredo finally spoke—in Bahasa Indonesia.

"Alfredo is curious. He wonders why they kidnapped Kuan Hee," Harry explained.

There was silence in the room. Everyone was in deep thought. Then Kuan Hee broke the silence.

"Might have something to do with my dad," Kuan Hee said. "The kidnappers might want something from my dad."

"Kuan Hee, have you heard from your father?" Tim asked.

"Not since I was kidnapped," Kuan Hee said. "They took my iPhone. By the way, where's my iPhone?"

"It is being charged," Lina said. "The battery has gone flat."

Kuan Hee put out his hand and Lina passed the

smartphone to him. He scrolled to see the call log. Several entries caught his eye.

"My dad called me," Kuan Hee said. "He's been trying to reach me."

"Did you tell Dad about me?" Kuan Hee asked Lina.

"Sorry, it didn't cross my mind," Lina said. "Everything was in a whirl. I didn't know what to do. I merely called Tim and Navin."

"It's alright," Kuan Hee said. He tapped his dad's number to call him. Soon father and son were in animated conversation.

"My Dad's in town," Kuan Hee said. "He's staying at Siantar Hotel."

"Where's Siantar Hotel?" Tim asked.

"It's only about five hundred metres away from here," Harry said.

"I've been here for four days, waiting for the kidnappers to call me," Professor Wang said.

"I'm OK, Dad," Kuan Hee said. "I am safe. In fact I am nearby."

"I'm glad you are out of harm's way," Professor Wang said in a voice thick with emotion. "Your mum will be so happy too."

Kuan Hee ended the call. "Room eighteen," he said. "Let's go."

Kuan Hee had gotten excited at the prospect of seeing his father again. He had forgotten they were in the middle of a discussion. He wanted to fly over to Siantar Hotel this instant.

The six friends could walk to Siantar Hotel, but it was faster using the minibus so they scrambled into the vehicle with Alfredo at the wheel. The minibus turned back towards the town centre.

Room eighteen was in the middle of a row of rooms on the second level of the Siantar Hotel. No one answered the door when Kuan Hee rang the bell. He knocked on the door several times.

"Dad has to be in," Kuan Hee said. "We just talked minutes ago."

"Perhaps, he's in the toilet," Lina said.

"Let's wait a little longer," Tim said.

The minutes passed and the knocking continued, still there was no response from the inside of the room. Harry walked down to the reception counter to enquire while the others waited outside the room.

Harry came back with a woman service staff. She knocked on the door and waited for a response before using a card key to open the door. Signalling the visitors to wait, she entered the room alone and returned to the door pronouncing the hotel guest was not in.

Despite protests from Kuan Hee, she refused to let them into the room. Then she promptly locked the door and left.

"Doesn't make sense," Kuan Hee said. "I was on the line with him just now. He said he would wait for me."

"Kuan Hee," Tim said. "I have a horrid feeling something's happened to Professor Wang."

"No! Can't be," Kuan Hee said.

"There's a CCTV camera overlooking the passageway," Tim said, pointing upwards at a camera perched in a corner below the ceiling. "There's no way anyone can steal past its eyes undetected."

"Let me handle this," Harry said. "I'll speak to the manager. Wait here for me." He and Alfredo disappeared down the staircase.

Just then, a figure appeared at the top of the staircase. He strolled down the passageway towards the group.

"It's Brigadier Walmsley!" Kuan Hee exclaimed. It was the Brigadier all right. Except for a slow gait and more wrinkles across his face, nothing had changed. He still had the same hunting hat, straggly beard and beer belly.

"Hallo Kuan Hee and Lina," Brigadier Walmsley said. "Fancy meeting you here—of all places. These must be your friends. Hi!"

"Mr Walmsley, you must be looking for my dad too," Kuan Hee said.

"Yes, afraid so," Brigadier Walmsley said. "Why are you guys standing outside? Isn't your father in?"

"We are trying to find out what has happened to my dad," Kuan Hee said.

"It's pretty stuffy here," Brigadier Walmsley said. "Why don't we go down to the lobby? It's much cooler there and there are seats too."

The Brigadier took the lead and the group of friends followed him down the stairs to the hotel's reception area. It was air-conditioned, unlike the passageway they were in earlier. Harry and Alfredo were at the counter with the hotel manager.

"Harry seems to be having difficulty at the counter," Tim said.

"What's going on?" Brigadier Walmsley asked.

"Mr Walmsley, my friend is trying to get permission to view the CCTV video footage for the passageway upstairs. We suspect something has happened to my dad," Kuan Hee said.

"I see," Brigadier Walmsley said. "You guys take a seat. Let me give him a helping hand." The Brigadier strode over to the counter.

"Will he succeed?" Navin said. "Harry and Alfredo are locals, yet have no luck."

"Don't forget he's an *Angmoh*," Lina said.

"So?" Navin said. "It's no longer the twentieth century. We're no longer under colonial rule. Being an *Angmoh* doesn't help."

"You spoke too soon, Navin," Tim said. "Look over there." The Brigadier was now standing next to the manager behind the counter looking at a monitor. He was also using his phone.

"He's an old hand at this," Kuan Hee said.

"I agree," Tim said.

Minutes later, the Brigadier returned to the group with

Harry and Alfredo. He took a seat next to Kuan Hee.

"Guess I came too late," Brigadier Walmsley said. "Should not have stopped for lunch before coming here."

"Did you see my dad coming out of the room?" Kuan Hee asked.

"Seems two men—of Chinese origin—took him away," Brigadier Walmsley said. "Just before you guys arrived. You were three minutes late."

"Three minutes?" Kuan Hee said in a tremulous voice. "We could have stopped them if we had hurried over."

"Kuan Hee, stop blaming yourself," Tim said. "Nobody knew these guys were coming for your father. Stop being hard on yourself."

"Your friend is right, Kuan Hee," Brigadier Walmsley said. "What we must do now is find your father as soon as we can—before he falls into danger."

"Mr Walmsley, what do these men want with my father-in-law?" Lina asked.

The Brigadier looked around the lobby. Then he turned his eyes on Harry and Alfredo. Finally, he looked at Tim and Navin. He seemed to be scrutinizing Kuan Hee's friends.

"Mr Walmsley, what are these people after?" Kuan Hee said.

The Brigadier leaned back on the sofa and twiddled his thumbs. "Shall we order some coffee? I'm thirsty."

A service staff brought beverages for all of them. In between sips of his favourite *kopi oh kosong*, the Brigadier chatted with Tim and Navin. It seemed he wanted to know them better. Both men had heard Kuan Hee and Lina speaking about the Brigadier so many times that they knew all about him and what he did.

"Who's he?" Harry asked Kuan Hee.

"Brigadier Walmsley is an American operative," Kuan Hee said. "My dad works for him. Mr Walmsley works for the American government. Special Forces."

"Special Forces?" Harry exclaimed. "Delta Force?"

"Right," Kuan Hee said. Harry translated their conversation to Alfredo, who looked in amazement at the Brigadier. Apparently, Alfredo had not seen a real American spy before.

"Kuan Hee, aren't we wasting precious time here?" Lina said in a low voice. "We should be out looking for your father."

"The Brigadier must have his reason for remaining here," Kuan Hee said. "Let's wait."

"Kuan Hee, I see you have been to the house on Samosir Island," Brigadier Walmsley said.

"Erh. Yes. Mr Walmsley," Kuan Hee said. "I was kidnapped and held there the past few days."

"I see," Brigadier Walmsley said. "Your friends have been there too?"

"They—they went there to rescue me," Kuan Hee said.

"Mr Walmsley, I went there too," Lina said.

"Lina, really?" Brigadier Walmsley said. "Gosh! You are a brave girl. Indeed very brave."

The main door opened and a tall Caucasian man with the demeanor of a warrior stepped into the hotel lobby. He walked over to the Brigadier and whispered into his ears.

"Kuan Hee. Apologies. I need to take my leave," Brigadier Walmsley said. "Have to settle an urgent matter." He bade goodbye to the group and left quickly with his escort.

"Just like that?" Lina said. "He's gone just like that. Without a word about your father, Kuan Hee."

"I know. I know," Kuan Hee said. "He'll be back—soon."

"But, he doesn't know where we are staying," Lina said.

"I think he does, Lina," Kuan Hee said. "For sure, he already knows what we have been doing on the island."

"Really?" Tim said.

"One hundred percent," Kuan Hee said. "He didn't look surprised when I told him I had been kidnapped.

Don't forget. He spies on others for a living."

"Why didn't we follow him?" Navin asked.

"We can't," Kuan Hee said. "We'll only be in the way."

"Maybe these Chinese men have taken your father to the island," Tim said.

"Yeah. Tim is right, Navin said. "Let's go save him now."

"Damn it, why didn't I think of it?" Kuan Hee said. "Are we too late?"

"Not if we go now," Tim said. "Everyone for it?"

The six friends nodded in unison.

"Let's go get our hardware," Tim said.

The sun was high in the sky when the speedboat cut through the calm waters of the lake, heading towards the same jetty the six friends had left that morning. This time everything was in clear view—the island with its lush vegetation and tall hills that jutted into the clear skies like the serrated edge of a knife.

At the jetty, the group left Navin and Lina behind to look after the speedboat. They were careful not to take out their rifles, for it was broad daylight and Samosir Island was teeming with tourists at this time of the day.

Climbing the hill was easier this time as the group was familiar with the terrain. Little Busy flew up to the house to provide them with an aerial view of the surroundings. There was no one in sight. The intruders readied their rifles and scrambled up the slope. When they reached the compound, they fanned out with Kuan Hee and Harry taking the lead in approaching the verandah. At one end of the verandah, the two men crouched down and kept out of view.

"It's eerily quiet," Kuan Hee said. "Like they are lying in wait to ambush us."

"Could they have abandoned the hideout?" Harry said.

"You mean they have taken my dad to a new hideout?"

Kuan Hee said. "Let's find out for sure." He raised his hand to signal to the others he was starting the search. At once, Tim and Alfredo aimed their rifles at the upper floor of the house. Both found each other unlikely partners; they were unable to communicate with each other. Both had to use hand gestures and hope the other could read the signal. A mistake could cost them their lives.

Kuan Hee and Harry checked the rooms one by one. Then they climbed the stairs to the second storey. The rooms upstairs were also vacant. Harry slung his rifle and leaned out of the parapet. He signalled to the others to come up. They were now all standing in the verandah on the second storey.

"The house is deserted," Kuan Hee said, dispirited. "It's only been half a day and they have managed to clear out so quickly."

"The rooms do not appear to have been lived-in," Harry said. "It is likely the kidnappers were using it as a hideout—nothing more. Once they were found out, they merely abandoned the place."

"But it's so big," Tim said. "Who in his right mind would spend so much money renting such a big place only to use it as a hideout?"

"You have a point, Tim," Kuan Hee said. "They might return."

"Let's see if we can find out more about the kidnappers from the things they left behind," Tim said.

"Alfredo will keep watch," Harry said. "Just in case."

Alas, they found no clues. Dejected, they trudged back to the jetty. Their looks told Navin and Lina plenty.

"Indonesia is so big," Kuan Hee said. "Where can my dad be?"

"He's got to be nearby," Tim said. "It's only been a few hours. He can't be far. We'll find your father." The others nodded in agreement.

49

CHAPTER 11

In their hotel room that evening, Kuan Hee and Lina received an unannounced visit from Brigadier Walmsley. The Brigadier lumbered to the balcony. He swept his hand in front of him. "Such a picturesque view. Kuan Hee, there are many more such views in this world of ours. So many that there's hardly enough time for us to enjoy all of them even if we visit one every day. Yet, man isn't satisfied. He wants to control the world."

Turning to face Kuan Hee, Brigadier Walmsley said, "Talented people like your father are always a target of unscrupulous villains in our world. These villains want to control mankind. It's been like that for thousands of years. Our history books attest to their misdeeds. Power is what they seek." He leaned towards Kuan Hee. "That is why we need to keep people like your father out of their hands. But it's difficult. These unscrupulous people attack your father's Achilles' heel—you—and force him to do things against his will."

The Brigadier sank into a cane settee and the weight of his back squashed the cushion, curling it inwards. He clapped his hands on his lap and gazed into Kuan Hee's eyes. "I'm getting on in years, Kuan Hee. I'm almost seventy-nine years old. Age is catching up with me. I can't do the same things I did three years ago when we last met."

"Mr Walmsley, you still look hale and hearty," Lina said. "You don't look your age."

"Yes. Lina's right," Kuan Hee said.

"Lina. My mind is young," Brigadier Walmsley said. "But my body is old—very old. His father is even older. He's—I think he should be eighty-one?"

"My dad will be eighty-one in January," Kuan Hee said.

"At our age, your father and I should be spending our twilight years taking care of our grandchildren. Instead, we are looking out for mankind. Your father has this special gift of knowledge. He knows it and he's been spending his entire life furthering his discoveries of the human mind and the technologies behind reproductive human cloning. He knows he is not a good father or grandfather in many people's eyes. But the fact is—his discoveries propel man into the future. He exists to help us live better." The Professor paused to collect his thoughts.

"Kuan Hee, do you understand what I'm saying?" Brigadier Walmsley said.

"Yes. Mr Walmsley," Kuan Hee said. "I've never doubted my dad's love for me. In fact, Mum and I always knew we had to share Dad with his work. He is his work and his work is he. We know it very well."

"Yes. That's right. Realising he hasn't got many years of his life left, your father copied his memories into an optical storage cartridge. You know very well, transcribing the data into another human brain is akin to creating another Professor Wang. Your father hoped, perhaps, some day in the future, you or some others could make use of these memories to further the progress of science," Brigadier Walmsley said.

"Was I kidnapped because of the mind clone cartridge?" Kuan Hee asked.

"Yes, I am afraid so, Kuan Hee," Brigadier Walmsley

said. "These men have evil designs for the mind clone cartridge. They will stop at nothing to get their hands on it."

"How did my captors know of it?" Kuan Hee asked.

"I'm not proud to say this—even our spy agency has moles inside working against our interests," Brigadier Walmsley said. "Your father is always a target for evil men who seek to control others. Yes. I hate to say it, but it's true. Man's greed is as wide as the ocean."

"So they wanted the mind clone cartridge in exchange for me?" Kuan Hee said.

"Yes. Kuan Hee. Your father travelled thousands of miles to come here to save you," Brigadier Walmsley said. "He snuck away when his minders were distracted. He didn't even tell me. That shows you are very important to him—more important than his work."

"Is the mind clone cartridge in their hands now?" Kuan Hee asked.

"I'm afraid so, Kuan Hee," Brigadier Walmsley said. "Both your father and the mind clone cartridge have fallen into their hands. Even if your father refuses to cooperate with them, they still have the disk. I believe the perpetrators have skilled scientists who can transcribe the data into a human brain. I seriously think they have the means and capability to do so."

"I'm curious. How do such things work?" Lina asked.

"Well, it's beyond me. But, in a nutshell, the neuro-scientist fortifies and impedes specially picked synaptic connections in the brain. This way, he creates and erases memories at will—at least that's what I remember the Professor telling me," Brigadier Walmsley said. "Kuan Hee, do you understand what I just said?"

"Yes. Mr Walmsley," Kuan Hee said. "Using some high-frequency light pulses, the scientist can stimulate synaptic connections in the brain, causing a change of state, thereby influencing memory. In short, it's memory control. A skilled scientist can manipulate a person's memories—for instance, erase, change or replace."

"Yes, Kuan Hee. Very well said," Brigadier Walmsley said. "You do take after your father. You've got his brain."

"Of course. He has," Lina said, beaming.

"Someday, we could use you," Brigadier Walmsley said.

"I'm nowhere near my dad in skills," Kuan Hee said, blushing.

"That's because you are still young, Kuan Hee," Brigadier Walmsley said. "You have untapped talent." He took out something from his pocket and thrust it into Kuan Hee's hand.

"With this you can return to Singapore," Brigadier Walmsley said. "Go back. It's not safe here."

"It's a passport," Lina said, grabbing it from Kuan Hee's hand. "A United States passport."

"Yes, with it you can travel anywhere—it's a diplomatic passport," Brigadier Walmsley said. "We give it to certain individuals who work for the US government. But it doesn't grant citizenship. That's another matter."

"You mean Kuan Hee's working for the US government now?" Lina said.

The Brigadier nodded. "It's time I take my leave. I'll get in touch with you shortly. Do you still have the walkie-talkie I gave you?"

"It's at home—in Singapore," Kuan Hee said.

"Never mind," Brigadier Walmsley said as he ambled into the corridor. "Goodnite. And don't lose hope."

CHAPTER 12

Loud knocks on their hotel door woke Kuan Hee and Lina that night. It was Alfredo at the door. His face was contorted in fear. He was rattling off long strings of words in Bahasa Indonesia. They had no idea what he was saying to them. He pointed to the next room. The pair looked inside—it was empty.

"What are you trying to tell us?" Kuan Hee said. He gave up talking to Alfredo and instead used hand gestures to communicate with him. Still he could not decipher what their Indonesian guide was trying to tell him.

"They went out? Why?" Kuan Hee said in response to Alfredo's waving of his hands. Clearly, Alfredo didn't understand a word he was saying.

"Alfredo wants me to follow him—at least, I think that's what his hand gestures are saying," Kuan Hee said. "You stay in the room. Something has happened to the others."

"I want to tag along," Lina said.

"Not this time, Lina," Kuan Hee said. "It's too dangerous. We're in a foreign land."

Kuan Hee grabbed his iPhone and backpack. He peeped inside the bag. *The Steyr AUG should do the job.*

To Lina's protests, he scrambled down the stairs with Alfredo.

Alfredo took the wheel and led the minibus out of the hotel compound into the darkness, with the vehicle's headlamps providing much needed illumination. There were hardly any streetlights on the long and winding road and it took Alfredo's driving skills to negotiate the bends without the vehicle veering off into the darkness. Kuan Hee did not know where the minibus was heading; he could hardly see the road. Even if there were landmarks, he had no inkling where he was.

Fifteen minutes into the journey, the minibus turned into what seemed like a plantation. There was row upon row of palm trees lining both sides of the road. The minibus came to a stop and Alfredo beckoned Kuan Hee to get down. He pointed to a row of houses ahead of them. In the darkness, they looked like a cluster of buffalo horns poking the grey skies. As the duo drew nearer, they saw wooden thatched houses on stilts. Two lampposts with light globes provided the only illumination in the area. Instinctively, Kuan Hee reached for the Steyr AUG. He readied his weapon as Alfredo led the way towards the buildings. The air was silent.

The two men were now at the corner of the nearest house. Kuan Hee patted Alfredo's shoulder and the guide turned to face him. Kuan Hee wanted to ask him where their friends were but didn't know how to do it. He stretched out open palms facing upwards, hoping Alfredo would understand. Alfredo pointed to the house in front. In his haste, Kuan Hee had forgotten to bring Little Busy along. The robot housefly drone could have allowed them to suss out the place. Now, they had to rely on themselves.

The men crouched between the stilts propping the house. Kuan Hee signaled he was climbing up to the verandah above them. Alfredo put out a hand so Kuan Hee released his grip on the Steyr AUG and clambered up the wooden pole. The rifle would have weighed him down for he was not good at climbing such things; he was not commando-trained.

Kuan Hee heaved himself over the wooden railing and steadied himself. He was about to stretch his hand for his rifle when someone grabbed him from behind. The man's heavy hands made light work of subduing Kuan Hee. It was then Kuan Hee realized there were two Chinese men, lean and mean, looking down at him.

"Run, Alfredo, run," Kuan Hee shouted at the top of his voice as the men dragged him away from the railing.

CHAPTER 13

There were loud knocks on the hotel door again. Lina grimaced. *Should I open the door? What if the kidnappers are out there? Kuan Hee said to wait. He didn't tell me what to do!* Her friends were missing and Kuan Hee had gone to look for them. There was nobody else that they knew here in Indonesia. Her mind was in a whirl.

"Kuan Hee. Kuan Hee. Lina. Are you in?"

It's Tim's voice! He's back! Lina rushed to the door.

"Why did you take so long?" Tim said, annoyed. Navin and Harry were standing next to him.

"You are safe!" Lina exclaimed. "You are all safe!" She let her tears fall.

"Why shouldn't we be?" Navin asked.

"What's happened?" Tim asked.

"We…we thought you were taken," Lina said.

"We merely went out for a drink," Navin said.

"Why didn't you tell us?" Lina said. "We were so worried."

"Our door was open. We saw the Brigadier walking past. We figured he wanted to have a long chat with you privately. So we thought we'd leave you guys alone with him. That's why we did not say a word," Tim said.

"We left Alfredo behind," Harry said. "Didn't he tell you? Oh! I forgot. He doesn't speak English."

"Alfredo?" Lina said. "But Alfredo said—I mean he gestured that something had happened to you."

"He did?" Tim said. "Where's Kuan Hee? Has he gone to look for us?"

"He and Alfredo left," Lina said. "Alfredo knew where you were."

"That's nonsense," Harry said. "Alfredo said he was tired, so we left without him."

"You could have called us," Tim said, waving his smartphone in the air.

"The phone! Why didn't I think of using the phone?" Lina said.

"How long have they been gone?" Tim asked.

"Er…about an hour ago, I guess," Lina said. "It wasn't long after the Brigadier left."

"Something has happened to Kuan Hee again," Navin said. Lina put her hands to her face and started crying. She wailed into Tim's shoulder.

Tim shuddered. The sudden turn of events was frustrating to him—to say the least. *Just when things are going right,* he muttered under his breath.

All eyes were now trained on Harry.

"He's a familiar face in Parapat," Harry said. "I spoke to my friends. They highly recommended him. I didn't know it would turn out like this. I'm sorry. Very sorry."

"It's alright, Harry," Tim said. "Nobody's blaming you."

"Did Kuan Hee take Little Busy with him?" Navin asked.

"Nope. He only took his backpack—with the Steyr AUG in it," Lina said.

"FindMyiPhone app," Tim said. "I forgot the iPhone's got this app."

Lina retrieved Kuan Hee's MacBook Air from a bag and powered the device. Then she stopped. She contorted her face and covered it with her hand. "I forgot. We haven't been using the FindMyiPhone app for years. Kuan Hee feared the government was spying on us. He deliberately kept off using it. We have been relying on Little Busy and Tizzy since." She was near tears again.

Tim patted her shoulder. "It's alright. It's alright."

"I tried reaching Alfredo," Harry said as he expelled clove-flavoured cigarette smoke. "He's not answering my calls." He stubbed out the cigarette and reached in his pocket for another.

There were many minutes of silence in the room as the four friends pondered the situation.

Then they heard a tap on the door. They had not ordered any room service. At once, Tim strode across the room to his backpack and took out a Steyr AUG. Navin and Harry followed suit. The knocks grew louder. With his rifle at the ready and Navin opposite him, Tim turned the door handle and let the door creak open.

"Gosh! It's Mr Walmsley!" Lina exclaimed from the far end of the room. The men relaxed their grip on their weapons.

"What are you young men doing?" Brigadier Walmsley said.

"Mr Walmsley, we thought—" Tim said.

"Seriously, do I look like an intruder?" Brigadier Walmsley said. Then he started coughing and fanned the air in front of him. "What smell is this?"

Harry flicked the cigarette in his hand and crushed it with his foot. "Sorry. Mr Walmsley."

The four friends crowded around the Brigadier. As he took his seat, Lina explained what had happened since he left earlier in the evening. The Brigadier rolled his eyes in disbelief. "Your lives are more interesting than a spy's."

The Brigadier twiddled his fingers. "Can someone get

me a *kopi oh kosong*?" he said. Lina called room service.

In between sips of the hot beverage, the Brigadier eyed the four friends—one by one.

"So this chap—Alfredo—took Kuan Hee for a ride and they didn't return?" Brigadier Walmsley said. They nodded.

"So Kuan Hee's got his iPhone with him?" Brigadier Walmsley said. "The one with the Polaris SIM card?"

Lina nodded. "Kuan Hee's been using this SIM card the past few years."

"Now, we have a way to locate father and son," Brigadier Walmsley said.

"Really, Mr Walmsley?" Lina said. Her face lit up.

Ignoring Lina, the Brigadier excused himself and plodded to the balcony where they saw him using his smartphone.

"I'm afraid I have to go," Brigadier Walmsley said as he pocketed his smartphone. "Lina, I will get Kuan Hee back safely. Trust me."

"Mr Walmsley, you found out where he is?" Lina asked.

"Let me handle it," Brigadier Walmsley said. Then he looked at the men. "All of you stay put. Hear? Don't be a hero."

Everyone nodded in unison reluctantly.

CHAPTER 14

What a turn of events! First, he was kidnapped. Then, his friends rescued him from the clutches of his captors. Now, he had landed in his captors' hands again. Kuan Hee shook his head as he pondered his misfortunes in the darkened room. *Alfredo will get help. Alfredo must get help. Where are they holding Tim, Navin and Harry? They don't seem to be here.* His mind was in a whirl. He opened his eyes. *Dad! Dad must be somewhere near!*

Kuan Hee shivered. He was unaccustomed to cold weather. In Singapore, he would pat his forehead and neck continually as he got about his tasks in the midday heat. He would wish for cool temperatures all year round. Here, he had gotten his wish, but he felt uncomfortable. It was colder than the air-conditioned environment he worked in.

It's too cold here. I must be in the highlands. I must be somewhere in Brastagi. Alfredo must have driven us back to Brastagi.

The door opened and the same two men ambled up to him. With his mouth taped, and his hands and legs bound, Kuan Hee was powerless to resist. One lifted him over his shoulder with the help of the other. With the heavy load bearing on him, the man shuffled into a corridor and then out into the open area in front of the house. It was even colder outside in the early morning air, but Kuan Hee took no notice; he had other things weighing on his mind.

The men unloaded their human cargo into a van and drove out of the plantation. There was no knowing where Kuan Hee's captors were taking him. *Perhaps, they are taking me to Dad. I will be meeting him soon.* As the van rocked along the uneven road, a sense of foreboding overcame Kuan Hee. It shook his consciousness.

About an hour into the journey, the van screeched to a stop. Then it moved again, albeit at a slower pace. Sunlight peeped into the back of the van through the opening behind the driver. It was noisy outside. Carhorns blared intermittently; loud voices rang out now and then. *I must be in some town.*

The van stopped again. This time, Kuan Hee heard the front doors creak open. Then the back door slid open and sunlight flooded the interior. The two men dragged Kuan Hee out into what looked like a room. *No! It's a garage, like the one in Harry's house.* Kuan Hee realized he was in a shophouse. The men heaved their hostage up a flight of stairs to the second level and into a room at one end of the building. Kuan Hee looked up at his new surroundings. He shouted at the top of his voice, but only muffled sounds came out. *Dad! Dad!* The elder Wang was right in front of him.

The men let go of their load and Kuan Hee fell onto the floor next to his father. Then they left. Kuan Hee crawled up to his father. He pressed his shoulder on him. The elder Wang glowed as he felt the warmth of his son's body on his. He too had been gagged and bound. Deep ridges of wrinkled skin formed along the edges of the duct tape fastened across his mouth. His eyes were heavy with sleeplessness. He was visibly tired and gaunt. His usually neatly combed hair was in a disheveled mess, exposing bald patches of scalp on top of his head. At his advanced age, he was too frail to take the knocks of captivity.

Though down-and-out, he flashed a weak smile. He was glad his son was unharmed. It had been a nerve-racking experience for father and son, and it was set to get worse.

There was so much that both wanted to tell each other, but all they could do was look into each other's eyes. They had to let their eyes do the talking for them. Both were not shy to let the tears flow down their face.

Gunshots echoed through the shophouse. Then came the sound of running footsteps and stomping. More gunshots rang out in quick succession. *Quick bursts. These have to be automatic rifles. Help is here!*

The Wangs huddled together under the window, their eyes trained on the door. Footsteps thundered in the hall outside. Then they drew nearer. The door flung open and a balaclava-clad figure towered in the doorway. He was wielding a Heckler & Koch UMP40 submachine gun. He shouted to someone outside and hastened into the room to cut the ropes bounding the two hostages. He beckoned them to follow him. Kuan Hee helped his father out of the room. With their rescuer covering them, they staggered across the hall to the staircase. At the bottom of the stairs was a slumped figure, lying in a pool of blood. A tall balaclava-clad man was standing next to the body. He waved them down. The smell of gunpowder punctuated the air. The garage walls and van were riddled with bullets. Another body lay on the floor. Father and son wobbled past it to the entrance.

Outside, a minibus was waiting with a third member of the rescue party at the wheel. There were faces peeping at the rescuers and hostages from behind windows and doors on both sides of the narrow road. But no one dared come outside; everyone was afraid of being caught in the firefight.

With Kuan Hee and his father safely in the minibus, the vehicle sped off, leaving the neighbourhood in a tizzy.

As the minibus cruised through the streets, the rescuers

took off their masks, revealing young, tanned and taut facial features. *Caucasians. They must be Delta Force. Brigadier Walmsley had come to their rescue again!*

The commando sitting in front of the Wangs retrieved something from his jacket and pressed it in Kuan Hee's hands. "I believe this is yours."

Kuan Hee beamed. It was his iPhone. "Thank you."

"We got your location with its help," the commando said.

The elder Wang leaned on his son. He was delirious. The ordeal had taken its toll on his health. Kuan Hee placed his hand on his father's forehead. "It's hot. My dad is having a fever."

"We'll arrive at our destination shortly," the commando said. "There will be a doctor to attend to him."

"Step on it," the commando in the front section of the minibus told the driver. The minibus accelerated towards Medan.

As the minibus pulled into a driveway, off a busy thoroughfare in the city, Kuan Hee saw the Brigadier, Lina and his *kakis* standing in the porch.

On hand to attend to the elder Wang was a doctor and a nurse. They promptly sat him in a wheelchair and pushed him into the building. The Brigadier followed them. The commandos straggled behind the Brigadier.

Lina flew into Kuan Hee's arms. She was delighted he had come to no harm. The others patted Kuan Hee's shoulder. They were grinning from ear to ear.

But poor Kuan Hee was in no mood to rejoice or answer their questions. Only one thing occupied his thoughts—his father's condition. He hurried into the building with the others tagging behind.

It wasn't a clinic or hospital they were in. It was a support centre that the United States government had set up to bolster its consulate in the city of Medan. The consulate, a stone's throw away from here, had been serving Indonesians in Sumatra since 1949.

"How's my dad?" Kuan Hee asked.

"Professor Wang has pneumonia," the doctor said. "There's fluid and pus in his lungs. We need to get him to a hospital straightaway."

"Go ahead," Brigadier Walmsley said. "I'll arrange security for him." The doctor nodded and excused himself. The Brigadier conferred with the commandos who had gathered around him.

"I'm going to the hospital with Lina," Kuan Hee said.

"We'll be at Harry's place," Tim said. "Keep in touch."

Professor Wang was admitted into the Intensive Care Unit at Rumah Sakit Polonia, a private hospital in Medan with English speaking doctors and staff. In the corridor outside the ICU, the Brigadier's two commandos stood watch, while Kuan Hee and Lina, looking forlorn, sat on a long wooden bench.

"Your father's in a coma," Brigadier Walmsley said as he emerged from the ward. He leaned over to place his hand on Kuan Hee's shoulder. "We have to prepare for the worst, Kuan Hee."

Lina burst into tears. "Oh. Kuan Hee. What shall we do? What can we do?"

Kuan Hee was a picture of calm outside, but inside he was crying his heart out. He was not one to openly display his emotions, but his wobbly voice betrayed his staid exterior. "I—I got to call Mum. Got to tell her."

The minutes stretched into hours. The Brigadier uttered some apologies to Kuan Hee and lumbered towards the lift; he had to get some sleep. The night was long and the wait frustratingly uneventful.

Lina curled up on the bench for some shut-eye, while Kuan Hee drifted in and out of sleep. He rubbed his eyes; he had to keep them peeled for news from the ICU. Then he slumped onto the bench.

Kuan Hee awoke with a jolt. He had heard his father shout his name. *Aiyah! I was dreaming.* Lina was fast asleep next to him and the commando on watch duty was at the far end of the corridor, leaning on the wall near the lift. Kuan Hee tapped the iPhone screen. It was showing 2:18 a.m. He took a deep breath. The air-conditioning was cold. He thought of putting his jacket over Lina, but realized he was not wearing one.

Then came the shuffling of feet along the corridor. Kuan Hee looked up. A doctor was rushing into the ICU. A nurse met him at the door. Kuan Hee's hunches went into overdrive. Goose pimples broke out all over him. He shook Lina awake. When the doctor came out of the ICU and approached him, Kuan Hee already knew what he was going to say—his father had left for a new world.

Lina cried uncontrollably. Kuan Hee wrapped her in his arms; he too let his tears run freely. It was a bad end to a long bad day.

CHAPTER 15

Morning came, gloomy and chilly. The dark clouds gathering in the sky outside the funeral parlour looked threatening. Another face of humid Medan was about to show itself.

The elder Wang's body lay in an open wooden coffin, bereft of embellishings and supported on a pair of short wooden benches laid perpendicular to the coffin. The hall was a non-descript one-storeyed concrete structure with a corrugated steel roof. The coffin took centre place, facing rows of benches and a wide entrance, flanked by folding metal doors. The parlour was typical of funeral parlours in the city.

Professor Wang was not of any religion, but he was not agnostic either. The scientist in him reasoned that the myriad intricate and delicate processes that supported life on earth were beyond the realm of science. So unlike the astrophysicist Stephen Hawking, who famously declared there was no god, he believed somewhere in the universe, some magical source had created the earth and every living thing on it. He believed life itself was a miracle and that the miracle was beyond man and nature. He believed somewhere out there, there was a superior life. Perhaps, it was God. But he stopped dwelling on this curiosity of his, for the scientist in him also argued that there had to be a scientific explanation for existence. With his death, the question of existence in his mind remained unanswered and his unadorned wake properly reflected this impasse.

"Mum's flying over," Kuan Hee said. "She won't be here so soon. Fort Bragg is almost two days away from here by plane."

"Kuan Hee. I'm lost," Lina said. "Terribly lost." It was the first time someone close to her had passed away. She didn't know how to handle the situation. Neither did Kuan Hee. Just how would one handle the loss of a loved one? Hours ago, his father was sitting next to him in the minibus, snuggling his warm body against him. Now he was cold and stiff in the coffin. Kuan Hee's thoughts drifted to the previous day's events—to the Chinese men who kidnapped him and his father. As their faces loomed in his mind, he boiled with anger. *Even if I have to go to the ends of the earth, I'll make them pay dearly.*

"Lina, I've never told anyone before," Kuan Hee said. "Dad and I were not close. He spent most of his time in his lab. It was his baby. I was not. But he came thousands of miles to save me. He died doing it. I hate myself. I really hate myself. I should have treated him better." His vision blurred as tears enveloped his eyes and drained down the sides of his face. Some landed in his mouth. They were salty. With tissue paper, Lina wiped the tears off him.

The rain came suddenly and in torrents. It whipped the metal roof, beating it relentlessly as if heaven was meting out justice on the perpetrators of his father's tragedy. How Kuan Hee's father would rejoice knowing heaven was on his side.

"Kuan Hee, why aren't you flying your father's body back to Singapore?" Navin asked as he and Tim joined the pair on the bench.

"My mum says it doesn't matter where we hold the funeral," Kuan Hee said. "My parents don't have many friends in Singapore."

"So your father's getting a quiet sendoff?" Tim said.

"It's what he wanted, really," Kuan Hee said. "My dad doesn't mix around. All he knows—and cares about—is his work. He never got around to making friends. He seldom received invites for weddings and gatherings."

Though the elder Wang lay lonely and lonesome in the coffin, his son Kuan Hee was in the company of his beloved life companion Lina, and his closest friends Tim and Navin who were here at the parlour to grieve with him.

Harry arrived with Uncle Kenny, bearing umbrellas, dripping wet. They paid their respects to the elder Wang before taking their seat on a bench.

"My father says you can stay as long as you wish," Harry said.

"Yes, Kuan Hee," Uncle Kenny said. "Find the ones who caused your father's death. Come to me if you need help."

"Uncle Kenny, these kidnappers may come looking for me at your house," Kuan Hee said. "You'll be in danger."

"Kuan Hee, I'm not afraid of danger. I have been through turmoil," Uncle Kenny said. "People came bearing lit torches. They looted my shops and then burnt them down. My friend had rocks thrown at him. He was hit with metal pipes till he died. He was on his way to his factory to save it from looters. Medan is no stranger to riots. We have come so far because we stick together. We go through weal and woe as one community. That's the reason why I'm around today. I'm alive because I never caved in." Uncle Kenny had gotten emotional. Kuan Hee's remark had triggered memories long buried in his mind. He was now reliving them.

Harry placed his hand on his father's arm. "Pa, it's the past."

"No. It may happen again, just as it did years ago," Uncle Kenny said. Lina passed a packet drink to Harry who placed it in his father's hand. Uncle Kenny's hands shook as he tore the straw off the packet.

"Why can't they leave us alone?" Uncle Kenny said. "We're only trying to make a living."

"Pa, it's over. Forget it," Harry said.

At that moment, Brigadier Walmsley stepped into the parlour. Drenched, he trudged to the side of the coffin to take a good look at his bosom friend. He took off his hunting hat, lightly shook off the water away from the coffin, and holding it against his belly, slid into a long silent conversation with the late Professor, shaking his head at times, and raising a hand to wipe his tears.

"Dad and the Brigadier have been working together for as long as I can remember," Kuan Hee said. "In fact, Mum says their relationship goes back decades."

"He looks very sad," Navin said.

"I believe Dad and he were best friends," Kuan Hee said. "Mum told me the Brigadier looked after Dad's interests well."

The Brigadier, having bidden a teary farewell to the Professor, took a seat next to Kuan Hee. He let out a long sigh. "Kuan Hee, I'm sorry that things have come to this state—very sorry. You see, after you were taken, instead of rescuing you straightaway, my men followed you, hoping your captors would lead them to your father." The Brigadier paused as if in thought. "But, never did I expect this operation would cost him his life. I'm sorry, very sorry, Kuan Hee."

"It's not your fault, Mr Walmsley," Kuan Hee said. "Those men dumped him in a room and left him to die. They're the ones responsible. They have to pay a price."

"Kuan Hee, let me take care of them," Brigadier Walmsley said. "Don't get involved. Return to Singapore after the funeral."

"Mr Walmsley, he's my dad," Kuan Hee said. "As his son, I have a duty to avenge him."

"But these are no ordinary men," Brigadier Walmsley

said. "They're professionals—sent by powerful people."

"Let me think over what you've said, Mr Walmsley," Kuan Hee said.

"Lina, make sure he doesn't get himself into trouble," Brigadier Walmsley said.

"I will. I will, Mr Walmsley," Lina said. Kuan Hee glared at her.

The Brigadier hauled himself from the bench and plodded to the entrance with Kuan Hee and Lina at his tail. Outside, the rain had petered out. The pair watched as the Brigadier, in his hunting hat, waddled into the back of a waiting car.

CHAPTER 16

After a day of rain, the skies over Medan cleared and the streets basked in the sunlight. The midday heat resumed its embrace of the city. In her haste, Kuan Hee's mother had dumped only the bare essentials in a Duffel bag, which she carried with her onto the plane. Tim and Harry met her at Polonia Airport and they arrived at the funeral parlour in Uncle Kenny's car.

Mrs Wang flew to the coffin where the Professor's body lay. She reached inside to touch his face and hair. She mumbled into his ears. She was crying inside her; she was not one to show her feelings openly.

Kuan Hee pulled Lina aside. He knew his mother wanted to be alone with his father. There were so many things that she would have to say to him. Kuan Hee had to let his parents have their last private moments together.

"Now that Mum's here," Kuan Hee said, "Dad won't be lonely anymore."

The funeral, which took place the next day, was a simple affair and the Professor's body was cremated in the afternoon.

"Your father left so suddenly," Mrs Wang said, staring into space. "I can't believe he's gone." Then she looked into Kuan Hee's eyes. "I've to return to Fort Bragg with your father's ashes. There is a memorial for colleagues and friends to attend. Once I have settled matters, I will fly home."

"Mum. I may not be home soon," Kuan Hee said. "Lina and I have to remain here for a while."

"Your father's gone," Mrs Wang said. "I don't want you gone too. Leave things be. Return to Singapore and wait for me. Besides, you can't be leaving Huei Huei with your in-laws."

"It's alright, Mum," Lina said. "My mother won't mind. In fact, she loves to take care of Huei Huei."

"Kuan Hee, did you hear what I just said?" Mrs Wang asked. Kuan Hee nodded. That was all he could do. It was the only thing he could do. He knew talking back to his mother would result in a never-ending tirade. That would bring her to tears and his plan would be ruined.

That evening, Kuan Hee's mother left Medan. She had no wish to stay longer in this place, which held nothing but bad memories for her. In her parting words, she pleaded with Kuan Hee not to disappoint her.

Kuan Hee was in two minds as he and his *kakis* milled around in the living room on the second storey of Uncle Kenny's house. Should he remain in Medan to track his father's killers and retrieve the mind clone cartridge that they had stolen from his father? Or should he do as his mother wanted—return to Singapore? He didn't want his mother to despair further. He opened the United States diplomatic passport issued in his name and flipped through it. On one page was an arrival stamp bearing a Polonia Airport immigration officer's signature and serial number on it. It seemed genuine. The Brigadier had everything arranged for him. He would be letting the Brigadier down too if he remained here.

"I've found him," Harry said, stumbling into the living room. "I know where he is hiding."

"What the dickens?" Kuan Hee said, as the four guests turned to look at their host, perplexed.

Catching his breath, Harry eyed the others in the room. "Alfredo! He's still in Brastagi."

"*Wah seh*, that's the best piece of news I've heard in ages," Tim said as everyone huddled on the floor.

"He's been staying with his sister in a village in Brastagi," Harry said. "If we hurry, we should be able to catch him."

"How long will it take on the road?" Tim asked.

"An hour or so," Harry said.

"It's already past eight o'clock," Lina said. "Will it be too dark out there?"

"No matter how late, I'll go meet him," Kuan Hee said. "You stay here, Lina."

"I want to go with you," Lina said.

"Shall we take the hardware?" Navin asked.

"We have to," Tim said. "Alfredo has an M16 with him."

"And my Steyr AUG as well," Kuan Hee said.

"My minibus's ready," Harry said, as he retrieved some flashlights from a cabinet in the room.

With everyone crowded into the minibus, Harry drove off. The minibus cruised past the city lights into the dimly lit rural roads towards Brastagi. It was a bumpy ride but the Singaporeans were no longer feeling nauseous.

After meandering along a track off the main road, the minibus came to a halt. The moon was conspicuously absent. The minibus's headlamps lit up the bushes in front of it. Elsewhere it was darkness. Yet Harry seemed to know his way around. Kuan Hee tapped his smartphone screen. At once, the OLED screen lit up showering light into the darkened surroundings. It was showing 8:23 p.m.

The occupants poured out of the minibus, slinging their backpacks and fumbling for flashlights. With Harry in front, they trod into the darkness. One by one, shabby huts appeared in the glow of the flashlights. These were

74

obscured by vegetation and sometimes, the five friends had to stumble along narrow paths. They were deep in a village, which lacked the convenience of streetlamps. Suddenly, Harry stopped and the intruders knocked into one another. He gave the signal for them to switch off their flashlights. Apparently, they had arrived at their destination. The home of Alfredo's sister was metres ahead of them, but it was pitch-black everywhere. Tim and Harry drew their rifles and prowled through the darkness.

The minutes passed slowly as Kuan Hee, Lina and Navin crouched in the vegetation. Mosquitoes were having the feast of their lives, delighted by the unannounced arrival of their human guests. The intruders cursed and swore as they scratched their necks, arms and legs.

Then ahead, leaves in the bushes rustled and branches snapped. Someone was approaching. The intruders froze. They were unarmed. In front of them, three figures appeared, two flanking one who seemed to be staggering. It was Tim, Harry and—Alfredo!

Tim and Harry let go of Alfredo and he fell onto the grass. Harry shone a flashlight onto Alfredo's face. The Batak native was distressed. Both Indonesians unleashed a torrent of Bahasa Indonesia, which pierced the silence of the night.

"What's he saying?" Tim asked.

"What are both saying?" Kuan Hee asked. They had to wait a while longer for their answer, for the two Indonesians were still in animated conversation.

Then silence reigned. Harry stared into Alfredo's eyes. It was some moments before Harry spoke.

"He says he needed money for his mother's hospital bill," Harry said. "He says he had no choice. His mother needed treatment."

"He could have come to us," Tim said. "We could have helped."

"That's what I told him," Harry said. "I believe he's not telling the whole story."

"Ask him who got him and me to go to your rescue," Kuan Hee said.

"I already did," Harry said. "He says an acquaintance brought a Chinese man to him. He didn't want to do the job at first, but the Chinese man threatened to harm his family. So he went along."

"Who's the man?" Kuan Hee asked. "Where can we find him?"

Harry rattled off in Bahasa Indonesia to Alfredo.

"He says the Chinese man who contacted him did not give any name," Harry said. "But he found out from his acquaintance the man's name is He Bin. He doesn't know where he is. But, he thinks his acquaintance knows."

"We've got to find his acquaintance first," Tim said.

"Question is—will Alfredo help us find him?" Kuan Hee said.

Harry resumed his conversation with Alfredo. Alfredo kept nodding. There was hope yet.

"Alfredo understands he needs to help us," Harry said. "He has no choice. Otherwise, I'll tell everyone in Brastagi what he did. He won't be able to make a living here anymore."

"Can we trust him?" Navin asked. "I'm not sure I want someone who has betrayed us around us. He could betray us again."

"Navin's right," Tim said.

"But, we've no choice. The acquaintance is our only lead," Kuan Hee said.

"Yeah, afraid so," Tim said.

"Then we've got to keep an eye on him," Navin said. "A real close eye."

"It's set," Kuan Hee said. "Harry, tell him we won't let him off if he tells on us again."

"Do we take him back with us?" Navin said.

"Yes," Harry said. "He's agreed to come with us."

"My Steyr AUG's with him," Kuan Hee said.

"He's hidden it somewhere," Harry said. "He'll take us

to it now."

Lina was most glad to be moving again. Those horrid mosquitoes had left itchy bumps all over her arms and legs.

With its human cargo laden, the minibus weaved its way out of the village and emerged on the main road.

"We're going to Alfredo's home," Harry said. But they did not visit the house. They stopped on a track behind the house. Harry, Tim and Alfredo alighted to retrieve the two rifles, which were concealed in a small shed away from the house.

CHAPTER 17

The sun peeped over the low buildings in Medan. As it made its ascent, its warmth enveloped the city and its rays shone into the windows of homes. Its glare caressed Lina's face and she opened her eyes. It was morning, yet Lina felt tired. She had not had her full forty winks. The previous night had taken a toll on her. She felt the mattress next to her. Kuan Hee was not in bed. *Has he left without me?* She shook off the blanket and strode out into the living room.

"Ah! You're finally awake," Kuan Hee said, looking up. He had been poring over a map of the city. "I'm studying the map. Need to familiarize myself with the city."

"Where're the others?" Lina asked.

"Downstairs," Kuan Hee said. "Did you think I was going to leave you all alone here?"

"You dare?" Lina said as she sat next to him.

"We're going to Sun Plaza, an old shopping centre," Kuan Hee said. "Alfredo's acquaintance works there—in the cinema."

"When?" Lina asked.

"After breakfast," Kuan Hee said. "Tim has bought some packets of fried *kway teow* from the market behind."

It was 10:00 a.m. when the men and Lina packed into

the minibus parked outside the shophouse. They had not taken along their rifles, for the Provincial Governor's Office was a minute's walk away from the mall; they didn't want to risk being found with firearms in the city. In Indonesia, unauthorized possession of firearms warranted a maximum jail sentence of twenty years. It might even attract the death penalty. But this did not deter many from carrying firearms. It was only a problem if they were discovered doing so. Even then, money quickly settled things.

The minibus pulled into the car park outside Sun Plaza, which was a walk away from Jalan Muara Takus.

Alfredo pointed to a middle-aged man in a plain blue long-sleeved shirt and grey pants, squatting against the parapet on the roadside pavement, puffing away at his *kretek*. He was oblivious to the happenings around him; he seemed deep in thought.

"Let's sidle up to him, pretend we are buying food from the cart vendor next to him," Tim said.

"Don't," Kuan Hee said. "We'll stand out like a sore thumb. Don't forget we're foreigners here."

"I'll go," Harry said.

"Look! He's got up. He's moving," Navin said.

"Let's follow him," Kuan Hee said.

"Looks like he's going back to work," Tim said, "in the cinema."

Alfredo's acquaintance entered Sun Plaza with his tail trailing at a safe distance. He took the escalator up to the fourth storey and disappeared into the Cinemaxx theatre. The posse lingered on the floor directly below, leaning on the glass railings and glancing up at the theatre entrance occasionally, but the man was nowhere to be seen. It was a fruitless watch that day.

"I vote we keep watch on this guy for a few days," Kuan Hee said, "till we find a lead."

"But, it'll be like looking for a needle in a haystack," Navin said.

"Do we have a choice?" Kuan Hee said. All shook their heads in agreement.

"This is a big mall, but we can't be standing here the whole day," Navin said. "People will take notice for sure."

"We'll take turns then," Tim said.

"The mall is about five hundred metres away from my house," Harry said. "It will be a breeze walking over."

It was Kuan Hee and Lina who were to do duty at Sun Plaza the next day.

"Let's take a *becak* there," Lina implored.

"But it's so near," Kuan Hee said. In the end, he hailed a *becak* and the pair scooted off, with the owner peddling the contraption from behind them and ringing a bell intermittently as the *becak* moved alongside hordes of motorcycles, with their horns blaring. It weaved through the traffic effortlessly, letting the pair take in the sights and sounds of the neighbourhood. They never felt this close to the road before; their feet were dangling inches above the asphalt.

"What if it rains, Kuan Hee?" Lina asked, peering at the flimsy canvas overhead sheltering them from the sun. "We'll get wet."

"Don't be silly," Kuan Hee said.

Upon arrival at the mall, the pair scouted for a suitable spot to keep watch on the theatre. Finally, they settled on a familiar name—Killiney—located on the third level. The Singapore homegrown coffeeshop chain had an outlet in Medan.

The pair took seats at a table overlooking the wide concourse, ordered coffee, and settled down for the long haul. Lina had brought along something to read. Kuan Hee, ever the perfectionist in whatever he did, proudly proclaimed, "I've got Little Busy with me." He placed the robot housefly and its remote on the small table. Poor AleXander the robots had to contend with the dark interior of Kuan Hee's backpack.

It was a good half hour before their target appeared. There he was, riding the escalator up to the fourth level. Apparently, he was still wearing the same clothes they had seen him in the day before.

Kuan Hee glanced around the shop before releasing Little Busy into the air. The robot housefly darted and danced forward and then flew upwards towards the theatre level. Then it disappeared out of sight into the theatre and the pair had to manoeuvre it using the remote.

They found the man, broom and dustpan in hand, pacing through a cinema hall, cleaning the place. Little Busy perched itself on a wall light to conserve power. The dim lights in the hall could not generate enough energy for the tiny solar panels on its body to absorb.

His work done, the man found a spot on a staircase landing next to the cinema hall exit and promptly made himself comfortable. In minutes, he was lying sprawled on the bare concrete floor, taking a snooze. Little Busy rested on a railing, not taking its eyes off the slumped figure.

"It's been a boring morning," Kuan Hee declared over the phone to Tim, who was back at the shophouse.

Lunchtime found the pair partaking of *mee siam* and *mee rebus* at the coffeeshop. Harry and Alfredo came up to them and took their seats.

"He's moving again," Lina said. The posse glued their eyes on the screen, watching their target move around the theatre. Finally, he appeared at the entrance of the theatre.

"Must be looking for food," Kuan Hee said. "Time for us to move too." He let the robot housefly hover behind the man and attach itself to his belt. "There! I've my hands free again." Then he folded the remote.

Outside Sun Plaza, the man approached a street vendor who had parked his motorized cart by the roadside. He was soon tucking into a bowl of *mee soto*. When he had finished with lunch, he whipped out his *kretek* and took long drags on it. Then he squatted down by the roadside and busied himself with his phone.

"This is frustrating," Kuan Hee said.

"Are we really going to be doing this for the next few days?" Lina groaned as the posse followed the man back into the mall.

All of a sudden, Kuan Hee stopped, and those behind him knocked into one another. Their target had turned back and was heading in their direction. *Good Lord! Has he seen us?* Kuan Hee wondered.

The posse turned their backs to the man, pretending to be in conversation with one another. But the man did not walk past them. Kuan Hee looked back. The man was nowhere to be seen.

"*Alamak!* He's disappeared," Kuan Hee said. They took to their heels, striding to where they had last seen him.

"Look! A door," Harry said. "He must have gone that way."

They scrambled through the door and out into a service road. There was no sign of their target.

"Drat!" Kuan Hee said. Then he realized Little Busy was on the man. *All is not lost!* He drew its remote and fingered the icons on the screen. "We have him. He's gone in that direction." They ran in the direction Kuan Hee had pointed.

"He's gone into Jalan KH Zainul Arifin," Harry said. "He's trying to hail a taxi."

"We need the minibus," Kuan Hee said. "We can't compete with a taxi."

"Wait here for me," Harry said. He grabbed Alfredo's arm and both men sprinted back to the car park where he had parked the minibus.

When he returned in the minibus, Kuan Hee and Lina got inside.

"The taxi went that way. It's a blue taxi with a bird on top," Kuan Hee said. "The map shows him moving along Jalan Pangerang Diponegoro. He's moving south towards Jalan Jendera Sudirman."

"Got it," Harry said. "Don't worry, I won't lose him."

"He's moved into Jalan Masdulhak," Kuan Hee said.

"I think I see the blue taxi ahead," Harry said.

"Yeah. That's it alright," Kuan Hee said. "It's the same toys hanging on the back window."

Harry stepped on the throttle and the minibus was soon tailing the blue taxi. "The taxi's turned into Jalan Walikota. It's—it's entering a car park. K-F-C. It's a KFC restaurant." Harry parked the minibus away from the entrance of the restaurant.

The KFC restaurant was a stand-alone single-storeyed building with alfresco dining on the side facing Jalan Walikota.

Harry pointed to their target. He was sitting under a big umbrella, enjoying his *kretek*. He kept looking at his phone. He seemed to be waiting for someone.

The posse took their seats eight tables away from their target.

"No need to be too near him," Kuan Hee said. "As long as we can see him. We've got Little Busy on him."

"Where's this place anyway?" Kuan Hee asked.

"We are near the Chinese Consulate-General's office in Medan," Harry said. "It's just around the corner."

As Harry spoke, a man ambled past their table. The man moved farther away from them towards their target and promptly took a seat next to him. He had his back to his watchers. They only saw he was short and stout.

"Time for Little Busy to do its work," Kuan Hee declared. He turned up the microphone in the robot housefly. At once, the remote reverberated with the conversation between the two men. They were talking in Bahasa Indonesia. It was Sanskrit to the Singaporeans so Harry did translation on the fly.

"He wants money from the stout man," Harry explained. "He claims Alfredo needs to run and hide from his pursuers."

"That's nonsense," Kuan Hee said. "Alfredo's right here with us."

"They don't know that," Lina said.

Alfredo rattled off something in Bahasa Indonesia.

"Alfredo says his acquaintance is lying through his teeth. He says they hadn't been in touch since the incident."

"This slacker must want easy money," Kuan Hee said. "He's a parasite."

"The other man is taking something from his pocket," Lina said. "I can't make out what it is."

"He's actually paying off the fellow," Kuan Hee exclaimed.

"How much?" Lina asked. But they were too far away to see the transaction. "Did they say how much?"

"Ten million rupiahs," Harry said.

"How much's that?" Lina asked.

"Five hundred Singapore dollars," Harry said.

"Only five hundred dollars?" Kuan Hee said. "That lowlife arranged my kidnapping for such a small sum?" He could hardly believe his ears.

"It's actually more," Harry said. "This five hundred dollars is a subsequent payment."

"Ask Alfredo how much they paid him to do the job," Kuan Hee said.

"Sixteen million rupiahs. Eight hundred Singapore dollars," Harry said, after conversing with Alfredo.

"That's a paltry sum," Kuan Hee said, "to play out a friend."

"Remember, Kuan Hee. Indonesia is a poor country," Harry said. "It doesn't take much to arrange a hit."

"The stout man is leaving," Lina said. "He's—he's walking this way."

The posse pretended to be in conversation with one another. The stout man veered near them as he made his way towards Jalan Walikota. He took no notice of them; his eyes were staring into the distance. They could see him clearly now. He was Chinese, fair and had a big beer belly. He was possibly in his middle forties.

It was the way the Chinese man walked that jogged Kuan Hee's memory. He took short swaying steps as he moved. Kuan Hee recalled seeing similar gait. *Now where did I see this?* Suddenly he realized the man was the one on the jetty shouting orders to his kidnappers on Samosir Island.

"He's the one," Kuan Hee stammered. "He's one of the kidnappers."

"What?" Lina said.

Alfredo mumbled something in Bahasa Indonesia to Harry.

"Alfredo says this man is He Bin. He's the one who threatened him into betraying you," Harry said.

"Quick! We've got to follow him," Kuan Hee snapped. At once, the group sprang to their feet.

"What about the other fellow?" Harry asked.

"Forget him," Kuan Hee said. "It's He Bin we're after." As the group strode towards the main road, Kuan Hee ordered Little Busy to detach itself from the Indonesian and return to base. Soon the robot drone was flitting over the remote in Kuan Hee's hand.

The posse's new target, He Bin, was about thirty metres ahead of them. He was walking along the side of a two-laned road lined with big trees, which hid the road from the sun's glare. There was a long line of motorcycles on the opposite side of the road, with scores of young Indonesian men huddled in casual conversation outside zinc-roofed shanties.

"I think he's heading for the Chinese consulate," Harry said.

Their target turned left and entered a gated compound, unaware he had been tailed. As the group approached the gate, they saw a single-storeyed bungalow with a thatched roof peeping over a row of tall bushes, which lined a low wrought-iron fence facing the road.

The group stood beside a huge tree with a massive trunk, pondering their next step.

"This is not the Chinese consulate," Harry said. "The

next building's the consulate." Harry pointed to a big three-storeyed building with an imposing portico jutting out in the middle. A gold ornate wrought-iron gate stood at both entrances to the compound, with a tall concrete wall, topped with ornate wrought-iron spikes, tucked between the gates.

"*Wah!* So opulent," Lina exclaimed.

"Is this a Chinese neighbourhood?" Kuan Hee asked.

"No," Harry said. "See the Indonesian men across the road? These men live around here. We Chinese live only in certain areas of Medan, like Jalan Muara Takus, where we're the majority. It's safer this way."

"You're saying, then, that He Bin is linked in some way to the Chinese consulate next door," Kuan Hee said.

"Likely," Harry said. "I don't see any other reasonable explanation."

"So, the Chinese consulate is smack in the middle of my kidnapping," Kuan Hee said.

There was silence in the group as they took in the severity of Kuan Hee's revelation.

"Let's go back to your house," Kuan Hee said. "We need to powwow."

"What about He Bin?" Lina asked.

"I think he's stationed here," Kuan Hee said. "In fact, I'm quite sure. We won't lose him. Let's come back another day."

CHAPTER 18

That evening, in the second storey living room of Uncle Kenny's shophouse, the four Singaporeans and their two Indonesian friends gathered. They snuggled down on cushions laid on the cold ceramic floor.

"We have to crack our heads over this matter," Kuan Hee said. "The Chinese government has entered the equation."

"People's Republic of China?" Lina said. Kuan Hee nodded.

"You are saying the Chinese government wants your father's mind clone cartridge?" Tim said. Kuan Hee nodded.

"That's espionage," Navin said.

"Did the Brigadier say anything about this?" Tim asked.

Kuan Hee shook his head. "I have yet to talk to him."

"So this chap, He Bin, you saw this afternoon is the same person who kidnapped you?" Navin said.

"For sure," Kuan Hee said. "My kidnappers thought I was unconscious, but the stupefying drug had worn off. I was as alert as any of them. It's the same man all right. Same clumsy walk. Same bloated face. His chin seemed to blend with his neck. I'll never forget his pudgy chin."

"Question is—who's this fella He Bin?" Navin said.

"We can assume he belongs to the Chinese consulate," Tim said. "He's got to be one of their employees."

"He's definitely not an Indonesian Chinese," Harry said. "He's a foreigner."

"Tim, google the Chinese consulate in Medan," Kuan Hee said.

"Already done," Tim said as he tapped on his iPad to bring up the browser. "Did all the work while you were still on the road. Here!" He laid the iPad on the floor for all to take a look. They huddled closer.

"The Chinese consulate office serves the different provinces in North Sumatra. Besides the Consular Affairs Office, it also hosts the Science and Technology Office," Navin said.

"Science and Technology Office?" Lina parroted.

"Yeah," Navin said. "I figure this He Bin you tailed is connected in some way to this office."

"He didn't look like a diplomat," Kuan Hee said. "More like a runner. Those men with him at the jetty looked like thugs."

"Probably they are the ones doing the ground work," Tim said. "We need to locate the point man. He is the one with the answers we seek."

"He must be the one who ordered the kidnappings," Kuan Hee said, his voice croaking. "He's the one who killed my dad." Lina grasped his arm and squeezed it gently.

"Could it be—these men are part of a triad, eager to lay their hands on your father's mind clone cartridge so that they can sell it to the highest bidder?" Navin said. "And the Chinese government is not involved?"

"It's possible," Kuan Hee said, "that these people are only interested in money. To them, it's just a commercial transaction. They gang up for mutual benefit. Their pay's much lower than ours. They have to find a way to feed their vices."

"We are guessing. We need more information," Tim said. "We have to recce the place."

"I agree," Navin said.

"Let me google a map of the road," Tim said. He opened the Google Maps app and typed the road's name. Then he switched to a street view of Jalan Walikota. He scrolled through the street. "Where's the house He Bin went into?"

Kuan Hee took over the iPad and dragged the images on the screen till it showed the bungalow. "That's the house. And this grand building next to it is the Chinese consulate."

"It'll be difficult not to be noticed," Harry said. "The shops opposite are frequented by young locals. You can't watch from there. You will stand out."

"Can we use your minibus?" Kuan Hee asked. "We can stake out the place in your minibus instead. See the cars parked along the road?" He fingered the vehicles on the roadside. "A minibus will not look out of place here."

"No problem," Harry said. "No problem."

"Harry, is it OK for you to be spending so much time with us?" Tim asked. "How about your shop?"

"No worries," Harry said. "My staff will look after it. Anyway, Chloe will be back soon. She can take over then."

"Who's Chloe?" Lina asked.

"His wife *lah*," Tim said.

"I forgot," Lina said. "She's visiting her parents right?" Harry nodded.

"We'll let Little Busy and Tizzy do the work for us," Kuan Hee said. "Little Busy will explore the house, and Tizzy will take a look inside the consulate."

"I'll take charge of Tizzy," Navin said.

"Why can't we go into the consulate?" Lina asked. "We can pretend to be looking for information."

"I've thought of it," Kuan Hee said. "But I don't want to take chances. These men may already know our faces. For sure, they can recognise me. They could have been watching us in Parapat or the funeral parlour. I don't want to alert them."

The next morning saw Jalan Walikota teeming with motorcycles. Hordes of young Indonesian men were ensconced on motorcycles and wooden benches on the sidewalk, chattering away amid the hum of motorcycle engines.

Harry parked his minibus opposite the bungalow, away from the rows of motorcycles lining the roadside. Alfredo was next to him. In the back, the four Singaporeans sat two abreast, peering across the road at the bungalow.

The bungalow looked lonely next to its neighbour, which had a steady stream of visitors the whole morning.

"It seems deserted," Lina said. "There's not a soul around."

"You spoke too soon," Tim said, pointing to a familiar figure sauntering along the sidewalk across from them.

"It's He Bin," Kuan Hee said. "He's got to be working here. I'll get Little Busy after him." He slid open a window to let Little Busy out of the minibus. It soared into the air and flitted across the road towards its target, He Bin. Soon it was no more in sight; it had disappeared behind the tall bushes with the Chinese operative.

On Little Busy's remote, Kuan Hee and Lina watched He Bin walk up to a man at a small desk in the porch.

"It's not really deserted after all," Lina said.

"Yes. There's someone guarding the compound," Kuan Hee said. He was giving a running commentary to the others who were seated away from the remote's screen. "Chinese. Early thirties. Close-cropped hair. Burly. Wait, there's something under the desk. It's—it's a short assault rifle."

"Let me take a look at the screen," Tim said. Kuan Hee held up the remote. Tim and Navin, who were seated behind the pair, analysed the silhouette in the image.

"QBZ-95," Tim declared. "A bullpup assault rifle used

by the People's Liberation Army."

"Why do they need assault rifles to guard the bungalow?" Lina asked.

"Might be something secretive they're doing inside," Kuan Hee said. "Otherwise, they don't need an armed guard."

"He Bin has gone inside the house," Navin said. "Quick! Let Little Busy go after him."

"All in good time," Kuan Hee said. "It's a small place. He can't go far."

"Yah *hor*," Navin said. "I forgot."

"No need to get excited so early," Tim said, smiling.

"Navin, I'm beginning to think my kidnapping is sanctioned by the Chinese government. It's not these guys moonlighting," Kuan Hee said.

"I agree. I made a wrong guess yesterday. You don't see moonlighters brandishing assault rifles in broad daylight next door to a consulate," Navin said. "The Chinese government must be behind your kidnapping."

Kuan Hee let Little Busy slip under the front door into the house. The remote's screen fogged immediately. As the robot drone acclimatized to the cool temperature inside the house, a wide corridor stretching the width of the house appeared on the screen. At the end of the corridor sat a large man next to the back door. He was guarding the door. There was a QBZ-95 resting on his lap. Little Busy flitted through the corridor to a window on the right. Its cameras peeked through the clear glass panel.

"It's a lab all right," Kuan Hee screeched.

"What?" Tim exclaimed, as he and Navin craned their necks to take a closer look. There were big pieces of equipment in the large room, which occupied half of the house. At the far end of the room, two men in lab whites were at work at computer monitors on a long table, flanked by racks of computer servers. Beyond them was a small partitioned area with glass windows. It was difficult to see what was inside.

"It's got robotic assemblers and DNA Molecular Assembly units," Tim said. Both he and Kuan Hee were specialists in nanotechnology, so they were familiar with the equipment.

"It's a cloning laboratory," Kuan Hee said, "albeit a small one."

"Yeah," Tim said. "Still, it must cost a bomb to set up."

"The evidence is piling up. It has to be a government operation," Kuan Hee said. "The Chinese government is behind my dad's death."

"Where's He Bin? Navin asked.

"He's got to be on the other side of the house," Kuan Hee said. He commanded the robot housefly drone to fly to the fork in the corridor. There were five doors in this part of the corridor—three on the side facing the front of the house. "The doors are shut and there are no openings under three of them for Little Busy to go through. We'll try the first door on the left."

Little Busy landed on the floor next to the door and crawled through the small opening into the room. On the remote's screen, a water closet loomed large above the robot housefly.

"Drat! It's a toilet," Kuan Hee said, as he manoeuvred Little Busy out of the small room.

"See if we have better luck with the next," Kuan Hee said as he let the drone squeeze under the door of the next room. "It's a changing room with lockers, a small table and chairs. There's a pantry at one end."

"We have to wait for someone to come out from the other three rooms," Lina said.

"Or go in," Kuan Hee said.

They didn't have to wait long, for the bungalow was a hive of activity today. The door opposite the changing room creaked open and a gaggle of men in lab whites poured into the corridor.

Little Busy darted through the air into the room.

"It's a conference room," Lina said. "They must have

been attending a meeting."

"Two more rooms left and both are at the end of the corridor," Kuan Hee said, as he let the robot housefly perch itself on the wall at the end of the corridor. "He Bin could be inside either room."

Finally, the door on the drone's right opened and out stepped He Bin and another man—middle-aged and bespectacled. Part of a desk and wall cabinet peeped through the opening in the doorway.

"Another office," Kuan Hee said. "Wonder who this chap next to He Bin is."

"Might be the man in charge of this place," Tim said. "Look at the way he swaggers in the corridor."

"Then he's He Bin's boss?" Navin said.

Little Busy darted above He Bin and the man as they walked towards the large room. The man looked into a square screen mounted on the wall beside the door. At once, the door slid open and both men entered, with Little Busy flitting overhead. The robot drone suddenly rocked and wobbled before recovering its balance.

"There's something in the air over the doorway," Kuan Hee said. "Something at the door could be spraying vaporized hydrogen peroxide to decontaminate visitors."

The room was alive with activity. There had to be a dozen people in it. He Bin's boss chatted with a wizened man in lab white as they stood next to the partitioned area.

Little Busy flew over their heads and hovered next to the glass partition. Its cameras took in the view of the room's interior.

"There's a man lying on a gurney inside. He's got a maze of wires all over his scalp," Lina said. "They connect to this big apparatus that looks like a hairdressing salon's hair perming machine. There are monitors around the room—like those you see in the hospital."

"His eyes are closed," Kuan Hee said. "Could be unconscious or sleeping."

"What are these men saying?" Harry asked. Though an

Indonesian Chinese, he didn't understand a word of Mandarin. The schools in Medan did not offer Chinese as a subject. His father spoke to him in *Hokkien* at home so there was no urgent need to learn his mother tongue.

"The man in lab white says the patient is in stable condition," Kuan Hee explained. "He says the transplant will be completed in two days."

"What transplant is he talking about?" Lina asked.

"Beats me," Kuan Hee said. "He used *yí zhí.* I think it means transplant."

"What kind of transplant takes two days?" Navin said. "A patient can die in the process. Perhaps, he means the operation will be carried out in two days."

"It's not what he said in Mandarin," Kuan Hee said.

"Let's not bicker," Lina said.

"Look! He Bin's boss is leaving the room," Tim said.

He Bin and his boss walked out of the house with Little Busy tailing them. They sauntered through the compound and out into the sidewalk.

The posse looked out of the minibus. He Bin and his boss were walking into the Chinese consulate next door.

"Let's go home," Kuan Hee said. "We've found enough information for today. We need to analyse our findings." He directed Little Busy back to its remote and the posse headed back to Jalan Muara Takus for lunch. Everyone was glad to get out of the minibus; they had been crammed inside the entire morning.

CHAPTER 19

Evening found the six friends in a room above Harry's provision shop. They lined the floor along the perimeter of the room, resting their backs on the wall, watching television on a wall-mounted screen as they discussed the happenings of the day.

"We still don't know the name of He Bin's boss," Kuan Hee said.

"But I can guess he runs the show there," Tim said.

"And there are so many men in lab whites," Lina said. "I counted eight."

"I think they are scientists," Navin said.

"The outside looks deserted," Lina said. "Yet it's such a busy place inside."

"Why did the Chinese government pick Medan for the lab?" Kuan Hee said. "Doesn't make sense. It's so laid-back."

"I guess it's a perfect cover," Tim said. "I mean, no one walking past the house would suspect anything. Their activities are so well hidden."

"And the laws are lax here," Harry said. "It's easy to get things done."

"I'm still trying to figure out what they are doing with

the man on the gurney," Kuan Hee said. "And why here of all places. Singapore has everything—the latest technology. And it's only an hour away from here by air."

"Just imagine, they take two days to do an operation on the man," Navin said.

"It might have been longer," Lina said. "We don't know how long he's had the wires on his head."

"Wires on his head," Kuan Hee parroted. "That's it. Why didn't I think of it before?"

"Think of what?" Navin said. "You're not making sense, Kuan Hee."

"The man with the wires on his head," Kuan Hee said. "He's undergoing a memory transfer process. They are either wiping his memories or transcribing new ones."

"You mean, like Colonel Tee and Jordan?" Lina said.

"Yes, exactly," Kuan Hee said.

"So the Chinese scientists are experimenting with memory control too," Tim said. "The same thing your father was doing."

"No wonder they are after your father's mind clone cartridge," Navin said.

"What did you just say, Navin?" Kuan Hee said.

"Huh?" Navin said.

"Navin said that's why they are after your father's mind clone cartridge," Tim said.

"That's it," Kuan Hee said. "That's got to be it."

"What?" Navin said. "You've got this bad habit of keeping us in suspense over your words."

"It's my dad's memories that are being transferred into that man's brain," Kuan Hee said.

"S-e-r-i-o-u-s?" Navin stammered. He sat upright. The others followed suit.

"That man lying on the gurney in the room is receiving my dad's memories," Kuan Hee said.

"He's like another Colonel Tee?" Lina said.

"Yes." Kuan Hee said. "My father's memories are going into his head."

"What you guys talking about?" Harry said. He was unable to keep up with their conversation.

"Now I understand everything," Kuan Hee said. "The Chinese government has got some willing scientist to be a guinea pig. It got my dad's memories transplanted into his brain." He paused in thought. "Horror of horrors! This chap can do what my dad can do. He is my dad—resurrected!" Kuan Hee's face reddened.

"We've got to stop them," Tim said. "With your father's knowledge falling into the wrong hands, there's no telling what evil they will do."

"We've got to terminate this man," Kuan Hee said. "At all costs."

A loud thud above them, followed by the sound of scurrying feet, sent goose pimples rippling down Lina's spine.

"It's rats," Harry explained, pointing to the ceiling boards. "There is a whole family up there."

"Don't tease her," Tim said. "She's very timid."

Lina leaned against Kuan Hee's shoulder, seeking relief, but he was oblivious to the distraction. He was deep in thought, plotting revenge.

"Kuan Hee," Lina cried out.

"Sorry," Kuan Hee said as he caressed her in his arm. "Sorry."

"We have to get rid of the man with the wires on his head," Tim said.

"Yes, we can't have another Colonel Tee in this world," Navin said.

"He's not another Colonel Tee," Kuan Hee blared. "He's my dad. My dad doesn't do evil."

"Kuan Hee, pipe down," Tim said. "Navin didn't mean it that way. He's right. Your dad's memories in this man's brain can cause a lot of harm to the world. There's no telling what evil these people are up to. We've got to stop them."

"That's what I mean," Navin said. "No offence meant,

Kuan Hee."

"I'm sorry I got all worked up," Kuan Hee said. Tears were welling in his eyes. "I never thought I would ever see my dad again. But this man has got his memories. He'll behave like my dad. It will be like seeing my dad alive again." Lina grasped his arm. She saw the hurt in his eyes as he grappled with the stark truth. He had to kill the man.

"Now we need to ponder the big question. Where's the mind clone cartridge?" Tim said.

"Yeah *hor*," Lina said. "We need to destroy the disk."

"Nope," Kuan Hee said. "I got to get my hands on it. It holds my dad's memories. His thoughts. His ideas. His lifetime of work—everything! I can't bear to see it destroyed."

"The mind clone cartridge should be in the house," Navin said. "They had to have used it to carry out the memory transfer."

"We need to go to the house again," Tim said, "when nobody's around."

"Night time's the best time," Navin said.

"What say you, Kuan Hee?" Tim said.

"OK," Kuan Hee said. "And we must work on the man on the gurney."

"What work?" Tim said.

"Perhaps, perhaps, we can reverse the process," Kuan Hee said. "Erase my dad's memories from the man."

"Do you know how to do it?" Tim asked.

"Er…nope," Kuan Hee said.

"You have no inkling?" Tim said. "Stop dwelling on this idea. We're running against time. We need to do the necessary."

"Kill him?" Kuan Hee said.

"That was the original plan, right?" Tim said. "You were the one who said—kill him at all costs, remember?"

"I haven't forgotten," Kuan Hee said.

"Look, Kuan Hee. He isn't your father," Tim said. "Your father's left this world. You've got to accept this fact."

"I know," Kuan Hee said. "OK. Let's do it."

"That's the Kuan Hee I know," Tim said.

"We'll go back to the house tomorrow night," Kuan Hee said. "We'll prowl the premises tomorrow night."

CHAPTER 20

It was a beaming moon that greeted the adventurers as they climbed into Harry's minibus. Having rested the whole day, they were refreshed and raring to go. So with weapons laden and the team seated, the minibus screeched into the dimly lit neighbourhood.

"Remember our mission's goals tonight," Tim said.

"Get rid of the man on the gurney," Kuan Hee said.

"Find the mind clone cartridge," Navin said.

"But we don't know what the mind clone cartridge looks like," Lina said. "Or where it is."

"We'll play by ear," Tim said. "I'm pretty sure it's in there somewhere."

"Lina, you stay in the minibus," Kuan Hee said. "I don't want to have to worry about you." Lina nodded. This time she did not protest. Kuan Hee already had a load on his mind. He had to save his dear father's mind clone cartridge. She shouldn't make matters worse for him.

"Navin, you keep watch in the minibus with Lina," Tim said.

"But I can't drive," Navin said.

"This isn't a heist," Tim said. "We aren't making a getaway. Also, the solar film on the windows is nearly opaque. No one can look inside. You don't have to worry about a police spot-check. Just stay in the back of the minibus." Navin nodded.

"I'll take Alex with me," Kuan Hee said as he fished the two robots out of his backpack. "Xander will stay behind."

"I'll let Little Busy follow you," Lina said. "So I'll know you are OK."

Kuan Hee nodded. "Don't worry. Everything will go smoothly." But the tremulous tone of his voice betrayed his rhetoric.

"Kuan Hee and I will take the front," Tim said. "Harry, you take the back."

"How about Alfredo?" Harry asked.

"He'll come with us too," Tim said. "We need all the hands we can get," Tim said.

The minibus pulled to a stop along Jalan Walikota. It was just steps away from the front gate of the bungalow. Except for a few cars parked along the roadside, the street was deserted.

"It's too bright here," Tim said. "People can see us from a mile away. Is there a back lane, Harry?"

The minibus moved along the road and turned left. More big houses came into view. Then a grassy patch of land loomed on the left. It was infested with unwieldy low-lying vegetation. On their left, bounding the greenery were houses. One of them stood out with its massive size.

"It's the Chinese consulate," Tim said. "The building next to it must be the bungalow." He pointed to a single-storeyed building adjoining the massive building.

"Harry. Stop here," Tim said, "in front of the overhanging branches." The vehicle slowed to a halt by the side of the road. "Prime your weapons."

With the bolts of their rifles snicked into position, the team dismounted and stole into the knee-high grass in single file. There was an uneasy sense in each of the adventurers as they prowled in the darkness.

They crouched past the towering consulate building and arrived at its humble neighbour. Then they sprang into action, stepping on one another's shoulders and hauling one another over the low concrete wall into the compound of the bungalow. Within the grounds, they stooped, looking out for CCTVs on the walls and pillars. Unlike its snazzy neighbour, which gleamed under big floodlights perched on towers, the bungalow glowed faintly in the light provided by small spotlights. But it served the purpose of the four intruders well.

The back door to the house was about two car-lengths from the wall where the intruders huddled, hidden by overhanging branches, pondering their next move.

"We're lucky these branches block the light," Tim said.

"I'll get Alex to neutralize the CCTV cameras," Kuan Hee said as he released the robot from its darkened quarters. Its front panel flipped open when he pressed a button on its back. At his command, Alex leapt across the compound and up one wall. Then it released a stream of laser beams, vaporizing the camera. With the job done, it ran across the wall to the other cameras, its tiny suction pads gliding it effortlessly over the rough surface, and put the cameras out of action in no time.

"Time to move," Tim said.

As Kuan Hee prepared to come face to face with the man who was usurping his father's memories, a sense of uneasiness overwhelmed him.

What if he has become Dad? What if he speaks like Dad? What should I do? These were questions lingering on Kuan Hee's consciousness. He shuddered to think of the repercussions of him facing off against this malevolent manifestation of his father. He might not have the courage to kill the man.

Tim nudged Kuan Hee on his arm. "Kuan Hee, time to move." Kuan Hee woke from his thoughts. "Sorry, Tim."

Tim circled the perimeter of the house. There was no one guarding the place. He returned to where the other intruders were kneeling in wait. At Kuan Hee's order, Alex burned through the back door lock with his laser beam. Then, one by one, the intruders entered the premises, rifles at the ready. The house was in darkness. The air was still and stuffy. They groped their way to the fork in the corridor. Then they fanned out, with Kuan Hee and Tim checking out the laboratory, and the Indonesians looking through the other rooms on the other side.

Tim produced a flashlight and shone it around the big room. Both men sidled to the partitioned room. Through the window, they saw the silhouette of the gurney. Kuan Hee opened the door. They saw nothing on the gurney. Tim trained the flashlight on the gurney. It was indeed empty.

"Drat! The man with the wires on his head is not here," Kuan Hee said.

Just then, Harry and Alfredo came up behind them. Their long faces told Kuan Hee and Tim what they didn't want to hear. The house was empty of people. *Had they got wind of tonight's operation? Did Alfredo betray him again?* These were thoughts running through Kuan Hee's mind as he stared into Alfredo's eyes. Alfredo rattled off a string of Bahasa Indonesia words.

"He says he has nothing to do with this," Harry explained. "He did not tip them off."

"Important things first, Kuan Hee," Tim said. "Find the mind clone cartridge first."

"My dad's mind clone cartridge must be in here somewhere," Kuan Hee said.

The intruders spread out across the empty house, ransacking the cabinets and drawers.

"One room left to check out," Kuan Hee said as the intruders moved to the last room on their right. "This is the one we didn't see the other time."

"It's only a storeroom,' Harry said. "Alfredo and I went

through it just now."

Kuan Hee turned the knob and they entered the room. It was big for a storeroom. There were tall shelves lining both sides of the wall with laboratory equipment neatly stacked on them. There were cell disrupters, desiccators and analysers. One shelf stored cleanroom wipers, frocks and facemasks. Three nitrogen generators lined the end wall.

"These are state-of-the-art stuff that they got here," Tim said. "This is serious stuff they are doing here."

"My dad's mind clone cartridge," Kuan Hee reminded Tim. "Find it first."

"Sorry, Kuan Hee," Tim said as the four men fingered the shelves and equipment in the room. They even checked the walls.

"It's got to be here somewhere," Kuan Hee said. "All the expensive things are stored in this room." He bent down to examine the floor. "Shine a light on the floor, Tim." But it was a futile search.

"We've got to go," Tim said. "We can't stay here for too long. Someone may come back."

"But we haven't found my dad's mind clone cartridge," Kuan Hee protested. "We didn't get the man with the wires. We found nothing."

"We'll find them sooner or later," Tim said. "Let's get out of this place first. We've been here too long." He slung his rifle, grabbed Kuan Hee's arm and ushered him out of the storeroom with the Harry and Alfredo following them.

Indignant at the prospect of failing their mission, Kuan Hee unleashed his fury, shouting commands to Alex, the last to leave the room. At once, the robot released a torrent of laser beams at the equipment in the room, burning to a crisp everything in it, and sending the place up in flames.

"We've got to make a run for it," Tim said. "The whole house is on fire." He pulled Kuan Hee out of the house with Harry and Alfredo flanking them, and Alex at their heels. In the compound, the four intruders came face to face with a Chinese guard, who had apparently been out on an errand. The guard drew a pistol from his waist and fired at them.

"Kuan Hee!" Alfredo shouted as he lunged forward. A hail of bullets dug into his back. He slumped into Kuan Hee, uttering something in Bahasa Indonesia.

Harry shot back at the guard, felling him. Kuan Hee knelt beside Alfredo, who was grimacing in pain. Kuan Hee kept shaking his head. "Alfredo. Alfredo."

"We've got to move," Tim said. "Help me lift him up." Kuan Hee, shaken by the sudden turn of events, turned somber. He heaved Alfredo over Tim's shoulders and the intruders staggered towards the rear of the house, to the back gate. Behind them, the fire was devouring the house. Flames leapt into the air. The air was intensely hot.

Alex's laser beam burned through the metal gate lock and the intruders scrambled into the darkness.

Suddenly, the bungalow was no longer a pale shadow of its brightly lit neighbour. The flames over it glared proudly over the massive building beside it. Like a supernova, the bungalow seemed to be enjoying a sudden burst of attention, before it was reduced to rubble.

Lina and Navin were waiting at the side of the road. Lina had been impatient, fearing the worst, when she saw the fire raging over the bungalow. She insisted on getting out of the minibus and Navin couldn't stop her. He did manage to hold her back when she tried to wade into the low vegetation.

Tim and Kuan Hee came out of the bushes, panting. A bleeding Alfredo was strapped to their shoulders. Harry appeared a moment later, bearing rifles on his shoulders.

The intruders bundled into the minibus, which sped off into the dimly lit neighbourhood.

"Quick, hide the weapons," Harry shouted from the driver's seat. "There may be police on the road."

Tim stashed the rifles below the seats, using some rags

to cover them.

"Is he dead?" Lina asked.

"His chest is moving," Tim said. "He's not dead."

"Don't say such things, Lina," Kuan Hee stammered. "He saved my life." He was frantically piling tissue paper over Alfredo's back. The Indonesian was incoherent and shivering. Kuan Hee's eyes were welling. He was feeling the strain of their failed mission.

"We're going to my family doctor," Harry said. "He lives three streets from here. We'll be there soon. How's Alfredo."

"I don't know," Kuan Hee said. "He's drifting in and out of consciousness."

"Look! A police van ahead," Navin called out from the front passenger seat. The occupants of the vehicle froze for a moment. It was Tim's quick thinking that saved the day.

"Here, pass me the tin of diesel," Tim said, pointing to the metal tin hanging on the rack separating the driver's section from the back of the minibus. Lina grabbed the tin beside her and handed it to him.

As the minibus slowed to a stop along the side of the road, Tim unscrewed the tin of diesel while the others looked questioningly.

"Surely you aren't going to pour it on the police!" Navin said.

"Boy! I must say. You do have great imagination," Tim said. "We can't have the minibus smelling of gunpowder or blood, you know." He poured diesel into some rags. He hung the rags on the rack. At once, the strong smell of diesel overwhelmed the air-conditioned air in the minibus, camouflaging all other smells.

"Kuan Hee, rest his head on your shoulder," Tim said. "Pretend he's drunk." He signaled to Harry to drive off. The minibus proceeded at a slow pace towards the roadblock. There were two policemen standing next to a police van whose strobing lights lit up the darkness.

A policeman waved the minibus to a halt. He ambled up to Harry, and with the deftness of a seasoned sentry, shone his flashlight into the driver's section and then into the back of the minibus at its occupants. He walked back to the driver's section.

At once, Harry fished some currency notes out of his pocket and pressed them into the policeman's free hand. He spoke in Bahasa Indonesia. There were smiles between him and the policeman, who waved him on. The Singaporeans' hearts skipped a beat as Harry stepped on the throttle and the minibus continued its journey along the darkened road.

"It's that easy?" Tim said.

"Yeah," Harry said. "Money is king here."

"What did the policeman say?" Lina asked.

"He asked what we were doing so late at night," Harry said. "I told him we'd just left a party."

"He didn't suspect anything?" Tim said.

"He only sees money," Harry said. "That's all he's interested in."

The minibus turned into a lane and pulled to a stop. Tim slid open the side door and helped Kuan Hee bring Alfredo down. Together, they hobbled towards the back of a shophouse. A man was waiting for them at the door. He led them through the corridor into a room where they carefully rested Alfredo on an exam table.

Then he cut through the shirt Alfredo was wearing and worked his way around his wounds expertly, looking out for entry and exit wounds. He turned him over and opened his mouth to check his airway for breathing. He pressed fresh gauze pads onto the four gaping holes on Alfredo's back. Alfredo was convulsing. He was suffering from shock as he had lost a lot of blood. With deft fingers, the doctor filled a syringe and plunged it into Alfredo's chest. Next, he tried to resuscitate him. But all was in vain. Alfredo was gasping his last breath. Then he turned silent. The long silence in the room was broken by Lina's sobs.

She had realized he had left them. Kuan Hee folded her in his bosom and let her cry in it. He held back his tears. He blamed himself for Alfredo's death. If only he had not been reckless that night. Alas, it was too late. But, whatever wrongs Alfredo had done, the Indonesian had redeemed himself by taking the bullets meant for him. Kuan Hee scolded himself for suspecting Alfredo had betrayed him again.

CHAPTER 21

In the minibus parked outside the funeral parlour where Alfredo's body lay, Kuan Hee and Lina sat. He could not summon the courage to enter the hall to pay his last respects to the fallen Indonesian. Tim and Navin came out of the nondescript building and boarded the minibus.

"Harry's with Alfredo's parents," Tim said.

"He's barely twenty," Kuan Hee croaked. "In the prime of life. Gone. Just like that."

"It's not your fault," Navin said. "Quit blaming yourself."

"Yeah. It's a twist of fate," Tim said.

Just then Harry emerged from the parlour. He climbed into the driver's seat and looked back at his friends in the back of the vehicle. "It's all done. Alfredo's family will take over from here." That said, he started the engine and manoeuvred the minibus into the traffic.

Kuan Hee was silent in the journey back to Jalan Muara Takus. In his eyes, two deaths in a week were too much to stomach. First, it was his dad. Now it was Alfredo. He wondered if his persistence would cost them more lives.

Back on the narrow kerb outside Uncle Kenny's shophouse, the remaining five adventurers lingered, leaning against the shophouse wall, or sitting on the parked motorcycles, staring into space. Harry flicked a smothering *kretek* stub into the air. It joined the dozen others littering the ground around his feet. The night was young, but they had too many things on their mind to enjoy themselves.

It had been a trying day for them. Kuan Hee had stared death in the face. Their mission was in tatters. It was Harry's first time witnessing someone dying.

"The mind clone cartridge must have been destroyed in the fire," Tim said.

"But we can't be sure," Navin said.

"Shall we stop here and return home?" Lina said.

"Let me think," Kuan Hee said.

"Your mother will be home soon," Lina said. "And she'll be worried sick if we are not home."

"Give me some time to decide," Kuan Hee said.

"Tim?" Lina said, looking at him for support.

"Guys, we came here to rescue Kuan Hee," Tim said. "That, we have done. And in all probability, his father's mind clone cartridge has been destroyed. There's nothing left here for us to do."

"Yeah. The police may be on to us, man," Navin said. "If we don't leave now, we may never get to leave. I don't want to spend the rest of my life in an Indonesian prison."

"And we may have worn out our welcome," Tim said. "We keep getting into trouble. I don't think Uncle Kenny likes the idea of Harry falling into trouble."

"My pa understands what we are doing," Harry said. "He is a little worried, that's all. Otherwise, he's OK with me hanging around with you. It's all right." In a way, what Harry said was true. His father was worried he would suffer the same fate as Alfredo. He was beginning to regret encouraging Kuan Hee to pursue his agenda. But he stopped short of telling the Singaporean visitors to halt what they were doing and return to Singapore.

"Shall we give it two days more?" Kuan Hee said. "Then we wrap things up and head home."

"Why, Kuan Hee?" Lina asked.

"Cos I want to find out what's happened to the man with the wires," Kuan Hee said. "He's got my dad's memories. I don't want him doing evil using my dad's memories."

"I plain forgot about the guy with the wires on his head," Tim said.

"Me too," Navin said.

"What say you guys?" said Kuan Hee. "We stay two more days. I promise we'll leave after that."

The other adventurers nodded in unison.

With long faces, the adventurers trooped into Harry's house. They settled themselves down on the floor of the second storey living room. Harry translated a newspaper article on the fire at Jalan Walikota.

"So it's just two short paragraphs on the fire?" Tim said.

"That's all they wrote," Harry said, holding up the newspaper in his hand. "See?"

"Nothing on the guard you shot?" Kuan Hee said.

"No mention at all," Harry said.

"The Chinese consulate must be anxious," Tim said. "They deliberately withheld important information."

"If the guard died, surely they had to report it," Navin said. "Did he die?"

"Everything was in a whirl," Tim said. "I didn't have time to check. In fact, I didn't even think of it."

"I think the Chinese consulate didn't want anyone to know about the goings-on in that house," Kuan Hee. "That's why they played down the fire as an accident." He paused. Then he continued, "We've got to keep a close watch on the Chinese consulate. Find out what happened to the man with the wires on his head."

"From the looks of it, the police won't be looking for us," Navin said, heaving a sigh of relief.

"Two things we've got to do," Kuan Hee said. "Tail He Bin's boss. He's got to know where the missing man is.

And find out just what they are up to. There has to be an evil scheme in this whole thing. I can feel it in my bones."

"Harry, when do you need to return the minibus?" Tim asked.

"No hurry," Harry said. "My friend doesn't need it back so soon."

"Let's go recce the consulate first thing in the morning," Tim said. "Shall we?"

"OK!" the others screeched in unison.

CHAPTER 22

Today, the Chinese consulate in Jalan Walikota was abuzz with activity. Next to it stood the lonely charred carcass of the bungalow that had occupied the interests of the adventurers the previous few days. Security seemed tight at the main gates. Milling around were men in plainclothes who looked more like members of the triad than visa-seeking visitors.

Little Busy hovered over the consulate's compound, giving the adventurers ensconced in the back of the minibus across the road an aerial view of the grounds. A covered car park stood on the left of the large building. The housefly drone flitted between two-storey-tall fluted columns adorned with ornate renderings emulating Greek architecture. It flew into a window on the second storey.

"We've got to find the man's office," Tim said. "Kuan Hee, throw up a picture of He Bin's boss." Kuan Hee swiped an image off Little Busy's remote onto Tim's iPad. Then he changed back to video mode on the remote.

"Let's see. He looks about fifty years old. Wears glasses. Broad face. Small eyes under bushy untidy eyebrows," Tim said.

"He's pompous," Kuan Hee added. "Remember the

way he swaggered in the house?"

"Yeah," Navin said. "Carried himself around like some VIP."

"Where's Little Busy now?" Tim said.

The robot housefly was exploring the corridors on the second storey. Its cameras captured some people seating on benches here and there placed against the wall. Some others were standing around, papers in hand, resting their arms or backs against the wall. On a wall, a TV screen perched, with a programme plying Chinese attractions to the visitors as they waited their turn.

The doors in the corridor took turns opening and closing, providing an erratic rhythm in an otherwise monotonous atmosphere.

The adventurers took turns manning the remote's screen. It was an hour later that something stirred their attention. On the remote's screen, a heavyset bespectacled man plodded into the corridor from the stairs. It was the same man on Tim's iPad. The man stopped at a door, inserted a key into a lock and turned it. Little Busy flew after the man and followed him inside the room.

The man settled himself in an armchair behind a small desk, next to a tall draped window. A nameplate on the desk read:

Cao Kun
Head, Science & Technology Office

Little Busy landed atop a tall cabinet across from the desk and the spies in the minibus prepared for the long haul.

"Finally, we know his name," Kuan Hee said.

"And what he does at the Chinese consulate," Tim said.

The morning was uneventful. He Bin's boss busied himself with some paperwork and phone calls. In between, he took a short nap. The minutes droned on for the spies

114

watching him on the remote's screen.

"He seems to be in a fit," Navin said. "Look at the way he slams things on his desk.

"Must be sore about losing the house next door," Tim said.

"Look! Someone is entering the room," Kuan Hee said.

"It's not He Bin for sure," Tim said. "This guy is tall."

The visitor's back was facing the screen. He slumped into a chair opposite Cao Kun. Then began a long animated conversation in Mandarin between the two Chinese men.

"What are they saying?" Harry asked. Like most Indonesian Chinese in Medan, he did not understand Chinese. Bahasia Indonesia was the only language he studied at school. Indonesian Chinese residents could only learn Chinese through private tutors, but Harry faltered in the language. It was alien to him and the family gave up trying to get him to learn the language.

Navin was in the same boat. Years of mingling with Chinese friends yielded some simple Chinese words such as *xiè xie* (thank you) and *bào qiàn* (sorry). Tim and Kuan Hee, though Chinese, fared only slightly better. They failed their Chinese subject at school. They were the *chia kantang* type of Singaporeans.

It was left to bilingual Lina to do the translation for the other adventurers.

"Cao Kun is telling the tall guy his superiors are angry that the lab has been razed," Lina said. "The fire has put everything behind schedule. His superiors want him to find out who's behind the attack on the lab. They want him to nab them."

"No wonder he has a black look," Navin said. "Serve him right."

"We still don't know who his superiors are," Kuan Hee said. "Someone high in government, I suspect."

"Remember. It's the Chinese government which is behind all the happenings," Lina said.

"That's what we thought," Tim said. "Now, I'm not that sure."

"Why?" Lina asked.

"We were hasty, jumping to conclusions. So much has happened recently. Logically—"

"Shush," Navin said. "They are talking again."

"Quick, Lina," Tim said. "Tell us what they are saying."

"I've got to listen first, right?" Lina snapped.

"Don't let's bicker," Kuan Hee said. "Lina, continue."

"They are making small talk," Lina said.

"It's going to be a long morning," Kuan Hee said.

"Cao Kun is telling the other man to look after things here," Lina said. "Says he's leaving tomorrow for Singapore."

"Did he say why?" Kuan Hee said.

"Nope," Lina said. "They are now discussing matters which need to be attended to here."

There was a knocking sound. The remote's screen showed the door opening and a stout man moving towards Cao Kun's desk. He stood next to the other visitor.

"It's He Bin," Kuan Hee said.

"Cao Kun is entrusting He Bin with an errand," Lina said. Cao Kun rose from his chair, walked over to a tall fireproof metal cabinet adjacent to his desk, and worked his hand at the combination lock. He opened the door and retrieved a slim rectangular metal box, the size of a paperback book.

"It's a hologram-encoded multi-mode ODS," Tim said.

"A what?" Lina screeched.

"What's ODS?" Harry asked.

"ODS stands for Optical Data Storage," Kuan Hee explained. "Essentially, it's 3D images storing vast amounts of information. It's an encrypted ultrahigh-storage device."

"That's a load of information," Harry said. "But I don't quite understand what you are saying."

"Kuan Hee is simply describing a storage medium—

like a flash drive, but stores a huge amount of information," Tim said. "Pay no attention to him. He likes to impress us with his deep knowledge and bombastic words."

"OIC," Harry said.

"Guys, you are interrupting my ears," Lina said. "I can't tell what they are saying."

"Sorry!" the men chorused in unison.

"Cao Kun's handing the ODS device to He Bin," Navin said.

"He wants He Bin to take the thing to Jakarta and hand it over to a man called Guo Wei at the embassy," Lina said.

"It must be my dad's mind clone cartridge," Kuan Hee said. "It's been here all along, not in the house next door. Why didn't I think of it?"

"From the size of the device, I can tell it contains exabytes of stuff in it," Tim said. "It can map the entire brain a few times over."

"Your father hasn't shown this ODS device to you?" Navin said.

"Never seen it before," Kuan Hee said. "My dad's always been secretive about his work. Even Mum doesn't know much about what he does."

"Does it mean you don't know how to repair AleXander if they are injured—I mean damaged?" Navin said.

"*Yah hor*," Kuan Hee said. "I never thought of it. I never thought they would come to harm one day."

"We must take good care of AleXander," Lina said. "We can't use them for dangerous missions any more, or we might lose them."

"Quiet!" Tim roared. "Listen to what they are saying."

There was silence in the minibus.

"I forgot to pay attention to them," Lina said. "Sorry."

"He Bin is leaving the room with the device," Navin said. "Shall we follow him or stay?"

"My dad's mind clone cartridge is more important," Kuan Hee said. "We've got to get it back." He commanded Little Busy to tail the stout man.

He Bin left the building and climbed into a car at the covered car park. Someone else was in the driver's seat. The car rolled out of the compound into Jalan Kalikota, sped past the KFC restaurant and turned into Jalan Polonia, with the minibus tailing it.

"He's going to Polonia Airport," Harry shouted into the back of the minibus.

"Huh? The airport's so near?" Lina said.

"We have to stop him before he gets to the airport," Kuan Hee said.

"The airport is two minutes away," Harry said. "There's no time."

"That means only one thing left to do," Kuan Hee said as he fumbled in his backpack. His hand emerged, clasping Xander.

"Surely, you aren't going to use Xander's rockets on He Bin," Tim said. He spoke too soon.

"What about your father's mind clone cartridge?" Lina asked. "All his hard work is in it. You can't just destroy it. You'll regret it the rest of your life."

"Hobson's choice," Kuan Hee retorted. "At least, having it destroyed is better than letting it be used for evil again and again." His mind was set. Lina knew it was futile trying to persuade him.

Perhaps, in his muddled mind, Kuan Hee had his answer to William Shakespeare's poser in *The Merchant of Venice*, the play that he studied in secondary school:

> If you prick us do we not bleed? If you tickle us do
> we not laugh? If you poison us do we not die? And if
> you wrong us shall we not revenge?

"I'll blow the car the smithereens," Kuan Hee said. "With He Bin and the mind clone cartridge in it." He pulled open the side window of the vehicle, unfastened Xander's front panel and uttered some commands to the robot. At once, Xander climbed onto the roof of the minibus and, standing with its hands on its waists and feet apart, fired a rocket at the car in front, blasting it to kingdom come instantly.

The minibus swerved to avoid the burning vehicle. There were more explosions as the flames shot up several storeys high. Pandemonium reigned in the street as motocyclists and drivers alike manoeuvred their vehicles to avoid the burning heap of metal.

"This time, I know for sure the mind clone cartridge is gone forever." Kuan Hee said, looking out of the back window with his *kakis*. "There goes my dad's life work."

"You have avenged your father," Tim said. "He should rest in peace."

"This is only the beginning," Kuan Hee promised. "I still have Cao Kun and his masters to deal with." Perhaps he had yet to hear Mahatma Gandhi's sobering words:

An eye for eye only ends up making the whole world
blind.

"Oh no. There'll be no end to this," Lina said. "Kuan Hee is fuming mad."

CHAPTER 23

Brigadier Walmsley waddled up to the four Singaporeans and their Indonesian friend as they stood on the kerb outside Toko Harry under the glow of the streetlamps. The air was cooler now but the heat of the day had yet to dissipate from the wall behind them. The adventurers had been waiting for him. He was, as usual, punctual. It was his trademark.

"Glad to hear you guys are leaving for Singapore," Brigadier Walmsley said. The Singaporeans smiled at him.

"Me too. Never did like this place," Brigadier Walmsley said. "There aren't any lifts. I've to climb the stairs all the time everywhere I go. At my age, it's a chore."

"Mr Walmsley," Lina said, "you still look fit. Should be no problem at all." The Brigadier beamed.

"Kuan Hee, come with me," Brigadier Walmsley said. He pulled Kuan Hee aside and both men took a stroll together along the roadside.

"Kuan Hee, you have caused enough trouble here," Brigadier Walmsley said. "Make sure you leave tomorrow. I won't be around to get you out of a spot; I, too, am leaving Medan tomorrow."

"Yes, Mr Walmsley," Kuan Hee said.

"Your father left some things behind in the hotel at Parapat," Brigadier Walmsley said. "My men picked them up while clearing the place. I've sent them to your mother."

"Yes, Mr Walmsley," Kuan Hee said.

"He also left behind a note," Brigadier Walmsley said. He fished out something from his pocket and handed it to Kuan Hee. "Here. I'm sure your father wants you to have it. Read it later, when you are alone." Kuan Hee nodded.

"Kuan Hee," Brigadier Walmsley said. "Those Chinese men whom you tangled with are not to be trifled with. One slip and all of you could lose your lives."

"But, Mr Walmsley," Kuan Hee said. "I've to avenge my dad's death."

"Let me deal with them, Kuan Hee," Brigadier Walmsley said. "I promise you I will make them pay for what they did to your father."

"Yes, Mr Walmsley," Kuan Hee said.

"There. I've said my piece," Brigadier Walmsley said. "When you have landed safely, give me a call—so I'll have piece of mind." Kuan Hee nodded.

The Brigadier got into a waiting car and waved goodbye to Kuan Hee. The car sped off into the dimly lit neighbourhood.

Kuan Hee unfolded the piece of paper and held it up under the streetlamp. It was a letter addressed to him. It bore his father's handwriting.

My son,

I had hoped I would not need to write this letter to you. But circumstances dictate that I should. I don't know whether you will get to read it; I don't know whether you will make it safely out of the kidnappers' hands. I don't even know whether I will get out of this alive.

All I know is, I've to tell you this—I have created a mind clone of myself. Remember the robot tank I showed you eight years ago—the one in the cellar of the house? In it exists my mind clone. It is essentially a copy of me minus the physical body. I've kept it updated regularly through the years using Polaris File Transfer Protocol. I didn't tell you earlier. I thought I would do it at a suitable time. Alas, I can't wait. The next few hours are crucial.

If I have to leave this good earth, I want you to protect the robot tank with your life. In it is my life's work. With it, you can help mankind.

Everything you need to know is in the robot tank. The mind clone cartridge I am using to exchange for your safety is a copy. The robot tank holds the master copy and more.

Take care of your mother, Kuan Hee. Take care of yourself, too. I am afraid I might not be around for Lina and Huei

Huei. Take care of them too. I love you.
Goodbye.

Your father

It was Kuan Hee's father's last words. He had scribbled them hastily just before the kidnappers paid him a visit in Parapat that night. Kuan Hee's vision turned blurry. It was as if someone had splashed water on his eyes. He wiped off his tears. He couldn't let the others see him cry. It would be unbecoming of him. But try as he might, his eyes stayed red.

Kuan Hee pocketed the note and rejoined the other adventurers who were waiting eagerly for him to update them on his conversation with the Brigadier. He merely waved them into the shophouse.

In the second storey living room, everyone sat in anticipation for Kuan Hee to begin talking. But he remained silent.

"What's wrong with you?" Tim said. "Were you crying?"

"Nope," Kuan Hee said. "It's the haze. It got into my eyes."

"Tell us what the Brigadier said, Kuan Hee," Lina said.

Kuan Hee took out the tear-stained note and passed it to her. She read it and handed it to Tim. The next couple of minutes went by with nary a word spoken as the adventurers took turns to read the note.

"I guess your father sort of knew he was heading into trouble," Tim said. "But, he didn't flinch. You were important to him."

"Yeah. Kuan Hee, your father was a brave chap," Navin said.

"I know," Kuan Hee said.

"All is not lost," Tim said. "Your father has the master copy of the mind clone cartridge." Kuan Hee nodded.

"You were so adamant to destroy it," Navin said. "Yet, it's still around. It's heaven's will. Definitely heaven's will."

"Yeah, Kuan Hee," Lina said. "Your father's work lives on. Use his knowledge to make him proud."

"Let's book tickets to go home, shall we?" Kuan Hee said.

"Yeah. Let's," Lina said. There was a chorus of approval.

"Harry, I'm sorry we've inconvenienced you and Uncle Kenny for so long," Tim said.

"What? Inconvenience? Nothing of the sort, Tim," Harry said. "It's been a pleasure hosting you."

"Come visit us," Lina said. "We'll show you around town."

"I will," Harry promised.

The four Singaporeans followed Harry upstairs to tell Uncle Kenny their decision.

CHAPTER 24

Flight MI234 left idyllic Medan for pristine Singapore with the four friends safely on board. Three of them had come to Medan seeking the fourth. Kuan Hee arrived in the city packed in diplomatic luggage. Today, he left it as a paying passenger on a commercial flight using a United States diplomatic passport. Such a twist in events, a staple in spy thrillers, followed Kuan Hee wherever he went. His life wasn't—ordinary.

The airplane landed on Changi Airport's third runway, used previously for military aircraft in the early noughties. The four friends deplaned at Terminal five, a mega passenger complex built in the late 2020s.

"So glad to be home—finally," Lina screeched.

"Yeah. We've been away too long," Navin said.

"No more *kretek* smoke following me wherever I go," Tim said."

"And an end to the honking and tooting noises in the streets," Kuan Hee said.

After breezing through the automated checks in the arrival hall, the four adventurers made a beeline for the shops. It was their chance to buy duty-free merchandise. Navin hunted for perfume for his mother. Tim headed for the alcohol aisle to get his father's favourite Johnny Walker Black. As for Kuan Hee and Lina, they were just glad to be together, windowshopping—their favourite pastime.

As they were sauntering under a humongous Moby Dick artpiece, something caught their eye. It was Navin's eagle eyes that alerted them. A chubby man was bending over a showcase looking at watches. It was Cao Kun! He had arrived in Singapore.

The adventurers were torn between wanting to go straight home to see their loved ones and following their only lead. It was Lina who spoke from the heart first.

"Huh? But I miss little Huei Huei," Lina protested. "I haven't seen her in ages."

"Look! Singapore is so small," Kuan Hee said. "He can't be spending a whole day travelling around Singapore. It'll only take us an hour or so. Be a sport, Lina."

"Our guy is moving down the travellator," Navin said. "Should we follow or not?"

It was Kuan Hee who lunged across the aisle after their target first. The others followed suit.

Cao Kun walked up to a taxi stand and took his place in the queue. Fearing he would recognize them if they stood behind him in the queue, the adventurers kept away from the taxi stand. Meanwhile, Tim booked an Uber ride with his smartphone.

"There's our ride," Tim said, pointing to a Mitsubishi Lancer, which had stopped at the road shoulder along the terminal entrance. The adventurers piled into the vehicle and sat waiting for Cao Kun who had now reached the front of the taxi queue.

Soon, the taxi Cao Kun was in cruised along the expressways into the affluent Bukit Timah district. It turned into Shelford Road and disappeared into a driveway at the end of the long road.

The adventurers remained in the Uber vehicle, plotting their next move. With the exception of Kuan Hee, all had luggage with them. If they disembarked here, it would be difficult for them to lug their luggage around Shelford Road, a magnet for upper-class residents. They would also stand out like a sore thumb.

"Let's see if he's merely paying a visit," Tim said. He asked the driver to let them wait in the vehicle.

There was no sign of Cao Kun after fifteen minutes. The Uber driver showed impatience, so the group decided to end their surveillance and head home.

"Never mind, at least we know where Cao Kun's living," Kuan Hee said, as their vehicle left for the main road.

With the adventurers safely dispatched to their homes, the Uber driver resumed his cruise for paying customers along the roads.

The first thing on Kuan Hee's mind when he reached home was to look for the robot tank, while Lina only thought of seeing her darling Huei Huei. In the end, Lina's tears won the battle, albeit for a short while only.

A day went by as Lina busied herself catching up with little Huei Huei at their house in Jalan Naung. Tim kept to his room, taking long naps to make up for the lack of sleep the past few weeks. Navin's mother kept him constructively occupied, discussing his wedding plans. She thought the sooner he settled down, the earlier he would stay put at home. In short, she thought it would get rid of his travelling itch.

What was Kuan Hee doing this while? He had rushed into the secret cellar to look for his father's robot tank, but it wasn't there any more. Instead, he found it nearby—it was sitting on an upper shelf of the bookcase in the study. Slightly longer than two palms of a hand, it was a scaled model of a main battle tank. He wiped the dust off with a cloth. It glistened. Its body was of a gold-titanium alloy, the same material that protected AleXander the robots. Then he got down to work on the tank. Try as he might, Kuan Hee simply could not get his hands into its innards. He was careful not to go overboard in meddling with the tank, for like his father's other robot inventions, it could possibly fire deadly live projectiles. He gave up in exasperation that evening. *What's the secret behind this robot tank?* His father's note left no clues; it had been prepared in haste.

Then Kuan Hee thought of his mum. Surely she should know how to unlock the robot tank's secrets. She was still in Fort Bragg in the United States, so he telephoned her. Alas, she too was none the wiser. The suspense was killing him. In desperation, he took to reading his father's note line by line, again and again, hoping somehow it would trigger some part of his memory.

"Take a break, Kuan Hee," Lina said. "It'll do you a world of good. Refresh your mind and then start looking at the robot tank again."

Reluctantly, Kuan Hee placed the robot tank on the desk. The pair passed time reminiscing their adventure in Medan. Just when they were marvelling at the rollicking good times spent there, loud beeping sounds interrupted their conversation.

The robot tank had sprung into life. It was beeping and whistling away on the desk. It took the pair by surprise.

"What happened, Kuan Hee?"

"The robot tank woke up."

"How did it happen?"

"Beats me. It came alive all of a sudden."

"But, we didn't do anything, or did we?"

"It could be something we said. Something either you or I said activated it."

The pair walked up to the desk.

"Gosh! The model soldier's eyes are beaming. I think it moved just now."

"Now what was it we were saying just now—before the tank started beeping?"

"You mean, something we said activated the robot?"

"Just what were we talking about?"

"We were just making casual conversation."

Suddenly, the toy soldier on the turret spoke. "At your command," it said.

"It's speaking to us."

"Why didn't I think of it before? Like AleXander, we talk to it. We give verbal commands to it. It can communicate with us verbally."

"But what activated the robot tank. One of us must have said something."

"Let me give it some commands. Let's see. What shall I say?"

Looking to the toy soldier, Kuan Hee uttered a string of commands which he had used on AleXander the robots. At once, the robot tank rumbled forward, then turned right and moved towards the wall.

"Stop!"

The robot tank halted in its tracks.

"It's responding to your verbal instructions, Kuan Hee."

"Yes, but for how long. Once it rests, I will need to utter its name again for it to wake up. But, we don't know its name."

"Think, Kuan Hee. Think of the names that we used in our conversation just now. That must be the answer."

"But we didn't mention any names—at least that's what I think."

"We must have said a name. The robot tank responded to its name being called."

"*Aiyah!*" Kuan Hee paused for a long while, trying to recall their conversation.

"I only said 'AleXander' once or twice, I think. I can't think of any other names."

He tried calling 'AleXander' but there was no response from the robot tank. An hour passed without any success. By then the robot tank had settled into a rest state. The toy soldier's eyes were no longer bright with light.

"For the life of me, I just can't think of its name no matter how hard I try."

"It's OK, Kuan Hee. Take a rest. Let's try later."

But Lina knew too well that it was no use telling Kuan Hee to give up. Once his mind was set on something, he would not stop till he reached his goal. So she got little Huei Huei to doodle on drawing block paper while she watched her. Kuan Hee settled into a long silence.

"That's it!" Kuan Hee's voice pierced the silence in the study.

"What? Kuan Hee. For goodness's sake, don't startle me and Huei Huei."

"Lina. I remember now. We were talking about AleXander. You were saying: AleXander. The great thing about—" The toy soldier atop the turret started moving again. Its beaming eyes flickered.

"There. The robot tank is responding to its name again."

"So what's its name? AleXander?"

"It's Alexander the Great, my dear." At once, the robot tank chirped and tooted again.

Lina's face lit up. "You're right, Kuan Hee. It's indeed Alexander the Great." The robot tank squealed a response.

"I never imagined Dad would come up with such a name."

"No one would think of it. They would be so confused. They would never think the name would come so close to Alex and Xander."

"Such an apt name for a robot tank. You know, Alexander the Great conquered much of the world then." The robot tank whistled and tooted in reply.

"See? The robot tank agrees."

"Now what next?"

"Find out how to access Dad's mind clone, of course. It must be inside."

"It will be like looking for a needle in a haystack."

"Yes *lah*."

Lina left Kuan Hee staring at Alexander the Great. It was time for Huei Huei to take a bath.

It was a good hour before Kuan Hee made his first move. He had spent the time visualising in his mind the possible ways that his father could have used to provide access to the robot tank's interior. He fiddled with the contraption, holding it in his hands and turning it upside down, fingering and pressing every part of it. He even tried pulling up the toy soldier. Still, he could not find a way to get inside. Frustrated, he put it down and sat gawking at it with furrowed eyebrows. *It's damned difficult to find out its secret.*

Then Kuan Hee thought of the Brigadier. *Yes, Mr Walmsley must have the answer. He knows Dad so well.* He contacted the Brigadier via telephone. Alas, like his mother, the Brigadier had no inkling. So it was back to the drawing board for Kuan Hee.

Kuan Hee was so engrossed that he didn't notice Lina slipping up next to him. "Any luck?" she said. Jolted out of his thoughts, he glared at her.

"You don't have to get angry with me, Kuan Hee. I didn't do anything wrong."

"Sorry."

"I was just thinking. Remember the tunnel at The Battle Box?" He nodded.

"Remember how we opened the tunnel door?" He turned to look in her eyes.

"Yes. We had to press two buttons simultaneously for the door to unlock itself."

"That's right, Kuan Hee. Is it just possible that your father designed the opening mechanism this way too?"

"Yeah *hor*. Dad was an iPhone fan like me. To grab a screenshot on iPhone, one had to press the side button and volume-up button at the same time. Perhaps, he used this idea on the robot tank too."

Kuan Hee pecked Lina on her cheek. "Thanks, dear." Then he went back to work, meddling with the robot tank again. He started from the turret and, using fingers of both hands, pressed every raised surface on the tank.

Soon he got to the front headlamps. He depressed both headlamps simultaneously. At once, two panels on the tank above the headlamps flipped open, and a screen rose, unfolding itself as it did so. The screen was now thrice the length it was. Delirious with excitement, Kuan Hee brought the robot tank towards his face and gawked at the screen. Then he placed the tank down and felt the screen with his fingers. *It's an OLED touch screen display.*

"Lina. Lina. Come quick!"

Lina practically flew into the study, with flannel in hand. She had been cleaning the stove in the kitchen. Seeing his excitement, she could not resist wrapping herself around him, wetting his back with the soiled flannel.

"Yikes! What's that on my back?"

"Sorry, Kuan Hee. I forgot. It's a cleaning cloth." She released her grip of him.

"My, really great job you have done. Fancy finding the secret in such a short time."

"Short time? My foot. It took me an entire day."

It also went on to take an entire night of his time as he tinkered with the hierarchical menu on the screen. He delved into the different layers of the menu and deep below, chanced upon one bearing his name. He tapped on the only file in it.

It was a video that played. In it, his father was addressing him. He listened in earnest in the privacy of the study. He came to the part about human cloning.

"You see, Kuan Hee. I can replicate a human body, but I can't grow a human mind. That part of the process of creating a real human being, though not fantasy, is still in the science fiction realm. That's why I call my creations clones, not human beings.

"My invention merely reads data off a human mind and copies these into another medium for easy transfer into another human mind. This is mind cloning. But to be sure, I can't call it mind growing. Mind cloning only maps a

132

human mind at a particular instance in time. So the information is dated. It is not updated in the sense it doesn't keep up with the growth of a human mind.

"But my mind clone is up to date. I continually update it with readings of my own mind and then upload these wirelessly via the Polaris satellite into Alexander the Great. There are about five petabytes of data, which represent a scan of my entire mind, in the Optical Data Storage drive. It's my gift to you. Keep it safe from prying eyes. Use it for the benefit of mankind.

"I know it's information overload for you. You're a clever boy. Play this video a couple of times, and you will fathom my intentions. Go to Brigadier Walmsley for help if you need."

Kuan Hee sat in deep thought in the silence of the night, digesting the contents of the video.

CHAPTER 25

The four adventurers pored over the map of residential Shelford Road that Kuan Hee had swiped off his iPad onto the large TV screen in the living room of 79 Jalan Naung.

"There's nothing for us to watch over in Shelford Road," Tim said. "It's only a residential area. It's where Cao Kun stays."

"I agree with Tim," Navin said. "We should focus on his workplace—the Chinese Embassy. Stake him out there."

Kuan Hee sat with crossed arms facing the TV screen, contemplating his fellow adventurers' remarks. He pursed his lips. "We are staking out Cao Kun because he has a secret to hide. So if it's a secret thing he is doing, do you think he will do it at the Chinese Embassy in broad daylight? He would be in pretence there."

"What if the Chinese government is in the secret?" Lina said. "What if the devious scheme is cooked up by the government? Then they will do it openly—at the embassy."

"I know. I know," Kuan Hee said. "But remember the house in Medan—the one next to the Chinese consulate?

They were carrying out some clandestine operation there. Perhaps, they are using the same method here too. They could be using the residence in Shelford Road."

"Logical assumption, but far-fetched," Tim said. "What was the first thing we did when we landed in Singapore? Head for home, right? That's probably what Cao Kun had been doing—heading for his home in Shelford Road."

"Let's stop bickering," Lina said.

"We aren't bickering, Lina," Kuan Hee said. "We are merely reasoning things out."

"Alright," Tim said. "Let's do it this way. We'll keep watch over both places. See what our guy is up to. But, we'll do it like this. Follow him wherever he goes. Not stake out the two locations. We don't have the manpower."

"Good idea," Navin said. "This way, we'll always be in the action."

"I vote we start with the Chinese Embassy," Tim said. "Wait there for Cao Kun to turn up." The others nodded their heads in agreement.

"The Chinese Embassy is not like its laid-back cousin in Medan," Kuan Hee said. "There are eyes everywhere in the compound. We have to be extra careful."

From Tanglin Road, the Chinese Embassy is an imposing sight. At first look, its fortified façade and overarching front gate entrance is a modern take on provincial gates in ancient Chinese cities. Granite slabs form a common theme, lining its façade and the perimeter wall along the road. Tanglin Road is a tree-lined two-laned road, which forks into a busy arterial junction serving the upper-class residential districts on one side and the urban shopping district of Orchard Road on the other.

The four adventurers stood at a sheltered bus stop across the road from the Chinese Embassy, pondering their next step.

"*Wah seh!* It's awfully big," Lina exclaimed. "It must be

at least four times the size of the consulate in Medan,"

"Yeah. It's huge," Tim said. "And it's on a slope. It will be difficult to watch this place without being noticed. I mean—anyone up there can easily spot us loitering around. There's hardly a soul out here."

"Let me release Little Busy first," Kuan Hee said. He opened his palm and the robot drone flitted into the air, glad to be soaking in the sunlight, its energy source. The drone flew across the road and up past the granite façade into the centre of the embassy grounds. The adventurers packed in front of the remote's screen.

The housefly drone landed on top of a CCTV camera perched on one of four tall spotlight towers on the premises. Its cameras beamed live pictures to the remote's screen, giving the adventurers an aerial view of the embassy.

"*Wah!* I was wrong," Lina said. "This place is six times bigger than the consulate in Medan."

"It's really big," Tim said. "It even has a swimming pool."

"Now, where is Cao Kun?" Kuan Hee said.

"He's got to be in one of these buildings," Navin said. "But, it will take ages to scour through them."

"Let's start work, then. Kuan Hee. Let Little Busy fly through the main building," Tim said. The robot drone flew past several large buildings and entered the biggest. It flitted through the corridors of the third storey, avoiding capture by CCTV cameras installed on pillars.

"*Alamak!* Why didn't I think of it earlier?" Kuan Hee said.

"Think of what?" Lina said.

"Cao Kun's Head of Science & Technology Office. This means he's got to be in the Science & Technology Office here too."

"Yah *hor*," Tim said. "Quick! Kuan Hee. Locate the office. We've wasted precious time already. We can't be standing here for too long. A few buses have passed us and we've not gotten on any. People in the embassy across the road will get suspicious of us."

At Kuan Hee's direction, Little Busy flitted from door to door looking for the Science & Technology Office. It was the third door on the second storey of the main building. The robot housefly crawled under the door into the room. There were four low-height cubicles in the room, which was about the size of a classroom. In each cubicle, stood an L-shaped desk. The remaining open space in the room held a round table and accompanying chairs. Little Busy hovered over the cubicles, one by one.

"Cao Kun's not in the first two cubicles," Kuan Hee said. "Let's take a look at the third." Little Busy flitted over the third cubicle.

"Kuan Hee. It's him alright," Tim said. Cao Kun was using the computer. The monitor was showing a page, which had Chinese words all over it. It was unintelligible to the three men.

Little Busy perched on a picture frame on the wall behind Cao Kun. Then Cao Kun's smartphone rang and he started speaking into it.

"Lina. Our Chinese is not good," Tim said. "We need you to be our ears."

"Sure thing," Lina said, smiling. She was happy she had a skill the others appreciated.

"I think the caller asked him to get the first batch ready in two days' time," Lina said. "He's asking for more time."

"First batch of what?" Kuan Hee asked.

"Didn't say," Lina said.

"Any names mentioned?" Tim asked.

"Nope," Lina said. "But, I think the call is from overseas. Cao Kun is talking about airport clearance for the stuff. Something about diplomatic cargo."

"So he's sending some stuff overseas," Kuan Hee said.

"Sounds like it," Lina said. "Cao Kun is speaking in accented Mandarin. It is difficult to catch what he's saying."

"He's put down the phone," Tim said. "Nope, he's calling someone now."

"He's relaying the earlier caller's message to the other party," Lina said. "He's telling him to hasten the work. By hook or by crook, the first batch has to be ready by Wednesday."

"He's put down the phone again," Tim said. "Kuan Hee, can you get Little Busy close to the screen? See what he's doing now?"

"No need," Kuan Hee said. "I'll zoom in on the screen from here. Little Busy's got telephoto lens." Kuan Hee tapped on the remote's menu and pinched the screen.

"Lina, do your work," Kuan Hee said.

"It's an air freight schedule," Lina said. "He's ticked departure for Thursday 8:00 a.m. Destination: Shanghai."

"So the stuff is heading for Shanghai?" Lina said.

"Seems so," Kuan Hee said.

"Look! There's a pickup ferrying workers into the embassy," Lina said, pointing to a blue vehicle moving through the front gate. "It says 'Johnson Painters' on the side."

"I know. I'll pretend to be a painter," Tim said. "It'll be better than loitering out here. Lina. Did you say 'Johnson Painters'?"

"That's what it says on the side panel," Lina said.

"I'll try to get into their team. I'm sure they need more helpers," Tim said.

"You sure or not?" Navin said. Tim nodded.

"Let me join you, then," Navin said.

Just then two uniformed men turned out of the embassy compound. They looked like security guards making their rounds along the perimeter of the premises.

"Let's get out of here," Kuan Hee said. Across the road, the adventurers shuffled along the sidewalk heading towards the busy junction. Minutes later Little Busy flew into Kuan Hee's hand. "We'll return tomorrow," he said.

CHAPTER 26

The Cherry Blossoms Apartments is a freehold property occupying two hectares of prime residential land in suburban Shelford Road. Once you enter the gate, you find yourself in a large garden replete with a winding driveway and dozens of large mature trees. A two-storeyed I-shaped building takes centre-stage. Its façade with arched French windows harks back to the colonial era, with its understated whitewashed walls, red-bricked pillars and an imposing gable roof. A porch, offering shelter from the elements for two cars, protrudes prominently from the middle of the building. But nothing in the premises gives any hint of association with cherry blossoms. Perhaps, some time in its past, there were many cherry blossom trees growing in its grounds.

Kuan Hee and Lina hunched on the floor in the back of a Fiat Doblo, a cargo van, which he had rented a day earlier. The van was parked on the side of Shelford Road facing the Cherry Blossoms Apartments. Apparently, Kuan Hee was adamant about staking out the place where Cao Kun stayed. While Tim and Navin were at work painting some part of the Chinese Embassy in Tanglin Road, Kuan Hee and Lina had planted themselves on Shelford Road.

They were keen on the secrets that the private apartments might hold.

"We've been here since 8:00 a.m. and Cao Kun hasn't come out yet," Lina said.

"Be patient," Kuan Hee said. "He has to go to work, right?"

"He might not be here," Lina said. "Then how?"

"Don't worry," Kuan Hee said. "Tim and Navin are at the Chinese Embassy right?"

"Yah *hor*," Lina said.

"Just relax," Kuan Hee said.

"I can't," Lina said. "I don't know why, but I'm getting the jitters."

"It's just your imagination, Lina," Kuan Hee said. "Don't worry. We'll be fine. We won't be in any danger sitting out here."

"It's getting warm and stuffy," Lina said.

"I'll let in more air," Kuan Hee said. He pulled the side panel door farther, making a bigger gap between it and its frame. "We can't be turning on the air-conditioning. People will know we're inside."

"I know, I know," Lina said.

Soon the two-laned road was receiving less traffic, signaling the start of a lull period until lunchtime. Most residents in the neighbourhood had left for work. But, nothing seemed to have stirred at Cherry Blossoms Apartments. There was no movement in or out of the premises.

"Can it be no one's living there?" Lina asked. There was silence in the van.

"Why haven't you released Little Busy into the place?" Lina asked again. She was getting impatient at the lack of progress in their stakeout.

"I'm doing it now," Kuan Hee said.

"Look! There's a car turning into the place," Lina said. The pair pressed their faces against the translucent glass window.

"It's Cao Kun," Kuan Hee said. "I was wrong. He's not living here after all."

"He's coming to work?" Lina said.

"Looks like it," Kuan Hee said. "There is more than meets the eye at Cherry Blossoms Apartments." He let Little Busy out through a tiny slit in the window. The robot housefly soared into the air and flew over the wall into the sprawling grounds, heading towards the moving car, which came to a stop at a covered garage next to the far end of the building.

Little Busy's cameras captured little activity in the compound. Except for one man, presumably a security guard, manning the front gate, it was empty of people.

However, inside the long building, it was a hive of activity. There were people—men and women—busily striding the verandahs and corridors.

"There has to be at least a score of people here," Kuan Hee said.

"But, we didn't see anyone coming in through the front gate," Lina said.

"Perhaps, they used the back gate," Kuan Hee said.

"There's a back gate?" Lina said.

"Don't know," Kuan Hee said. "We'll find out afterwards. Let's follow Cao Kun first."

"No need to wait. I'll fly Tizzy into the place," Lina said. "It will find out for sure." She released Tizzy the robot dragonfly into the air outside the van. It flitted over the young trees on the sidewalk into the apartments. It flew over the compound towards the perimeter fencing beyond it, looking for a gate. Finally, it found one behind the long building. The metal grille gate was at the bottom of a slope, level with the basement floor of the building. There was someone sitting at a small table on a verandah. He seemed to be watching the back gate.

"They must have come in through the back gate," Kuan Hee said. "It's strange that they don't use the front gate. Very strange indeed."

"Perhaps, they don't want to attract attention," Lina said. "After all, this is a residential estate." She let Tizzy land on a small tree near the gate.

"Now we have more eyes on the compound," Lina proudly declared.

"These people are up to something," Kuan Hee said. "It's beginning to look like a factory here."

"The whole building is air-conditioned, Kuan Hee," Lina said, glancing at the temperature gauge on Little Busy's remote. "Where's Cao Kun?"

"We were so busy sussing out the back gate, I plain forgot about him," Kuan Hee said. "He was at this spot just now." He manoeuvred Little Busy through the corridor on the first storey. Then the robot housefly flitted past a lift and up the staircase at the end of the building. On the second storey, its cameras saw a set of double-leaved glass doors adjacent to the lift. It led to an entire floor of platformed workspace stretching all the way to the other end of the building. There were men and women in lab whites at work on big machines here and there.

"I was wrong. It's not a factory after all," Kuan Hee said. "It's a lab—and a very big one. We'll wait for someone to let Little Busy in."

It wasn't a long wait, for every few minutes, the doors flipped open automatically when someone went near it. Little Busy took the chance to slip in unnoticed. It wobbled and wavered before balancing itself and then fluttered through the large laboratory.

There were all sorts of equipment, ranging from the very small to the very large—DNA stabilisers, scanning electron microscopes, spectrometers, nitrogen generators, multi-purpose X-Ray diffractometers, cryogenic systems, tissue replicators and fabrication systems—the works!

There were several partitioned areas, one of which looked like an operating theatre in a hospital with its large operating table and overhead lights. On one side in the room were electrocautery machines and tanks containing possibly oxygen or anaesthetic gases. Some men and women in lab white uniforms crowded around the operating table. It was difficult to see what they were doing. Standing outside the operating theatre were robotic assemblers and DNA Molecular Assembly units.

Along one wall of the laboratory was a nest of servers on racks. Next to them, on long tables laid against the wall were computer monitors and keyboards. More men and women were at work here.

It was indeed a big operation unlike any other that Kuan Hee and Lina had laid eyes on.

"Such a large-scale operation only means one thing," Kuan Hee said. "People at the top of the Chinese government are involved."

"It's way over our head," Lina said. "We're powerless against them, Kuan Hee. Shall we get help?"

"You mean, Brigadier Walmsley?" Kuan Hee said.

"Yes. He's the only one who can handle them," Lina said. "He's got the United States government behind him."

"Let's get more evidence before we alert the Brigadier," Kuan Hee said. "I want to be sure first. I want to find out exactly what these guys are up to." Lina nodded.

"By the way, where's that guy Cao Kun?" Kuan Hee said. "I don't see him anywhere."

"Try downstairs again, Kuan Hee," Lina said. Little Busy flew behind a man in lab white and followed him out of the laboratory.

Downstairs, the robot housefly flitted from door to door, looking for openings under the door. But it found none. The pair resigned themselves to letting Little Busy perch itself atop a CCTV camera mounted on the wall.

It wasn't long before a door below the robot housefly opened and out stepped a familiar face. It was Cao Kun all right. Little Busy hovered above the Chinese man, following him as he lumbered along the corridor, carrying some files in one hand. He entered a room at the end of the corridor with Little Busy at his tail.

It was a large room with a long table and a dozen chairs. There was no one else in it. He strode to the head of the table, dumped the files on it and slumped into the chair.

Minutes passed. Some men and women in lab whites streamed into the room and took their seats. When all the seats were occupied, Cao Kun started speaking.

"What's he saying?" Kuan Hee asked.

"Shush!" Lina said. "Let me hear some more first." She scribbled on a notepad as she listened to the meeting.

"Lina, tell me what they are saying," Kuan Hee snapped. He was getting impatient.

At last, Lina spoke. "They are discussing a delivery schedule for human clones."

"Human clones?" Kuan Hee parroted.

"That's what Cao Kun is saying. They have to get ready eight human clones over the next four weeks."

Just then, the door opened and a man in a wheelchair entered. He wheeled himself to an unoccupied space along the table.

"It's him. It's the man on the gurney in the house," Kuan Hee stammered.

"You mean the one with the wires on his head?" Lina said.

"Yes. But, he's in a wheelchair this time," Kuan Hee said.

"Shush!" Lina said. "Let me listen in to their conversation."

There was silence in the van for the next few minutes.

"The man in the wheelchair," Lina said. "His name is Wei Xin. He is telling the others the mind swapping is on schedule."

"He—his mannerisms are familiar," Kuan Hee said. "He gestures like my dad."

"Remember? He's got your dad's mind," Lina said. "They cloned your father's mind into his brain."

"But, he's not my dad," Kuan Hee said. "I've got to

destroy him before he commits more evil."

"Are you serious?" Lina said. "You want to kill him?" Kuan Hee nodded. "What about your father's mind. It is in his brain. If he dies, your father dies too."

"I've got my dad's mind clone data in the robot tank," Kuan Hee said. "My dad's memories are safe."

"Oh! I forgot about that," Lina said. "But, we still don't know how to make use of it, Kuan Hee."

"I can ask the Brigadier for help," Kuan Hee said. "He's got a whole lab behind him—and my dad's staff too."

"We've been here ages, Kuan Hee," Lina said, fisting her bended knees. "I'm hot and tired."

"Time to pick up Tim and Navin at Tanglin Road," Kuan Hee said. "Let's go."

The pair made an awkward attempt to get down from the back of the van. They had been sitting for hours and their legs were numb from inactivity. They climbed into the driver's section and Kuan Hee set the vehicle to autonomous mode. He tapped Tanglin Road on a virtual map on the front panel. Then they settled down in the cool airconditioning as the vehicle cruised down Shelford Road and turned into Bukit Timah Road.

On autonomous mode, the van moved at a leisurely pace as it negotiated traffic along the roads, but the pair did not complain. They were not in a hurry to get to their destination. They were relishing the air-conditioning.

Kuan Hee took over the wheel along Tanglin Road. Tim and Navin were waiting for them along the sidewalk. They had gotten down from the contractor's pickup when it left the embassy. The two men slumped into the back of the van, resting against its frame and the van resumed its journey.

Lina broke the silence. "Did you guys find out anything at the embassy?"

"Give us a minute to cool down," Tim said. "No. Five minutes."

"I've never been so tired before," Navin said.

"Yeah. It was solid work, painting the swimming pool area," Tim added. "It was hot, real hot. The reflection from the water in the pool made things worse. I think I'm having a headache now."

"Gosh! It's not that bad," Kuan Hee said. "You guys are army trained, you know."

"What's that got to do with painting the place?" Navin said. "It was sheer hard work. My muscles are aching."

"I thought it was a simple job," Kuan Hee said.

"Next time, you do it," Tim said. "Then you'll know."

"OK, guys. Quit bickering," Lina said. "So what did you find out?"

"We didn't get to see Cao Kun the whole day," Navin said. "Perhaps, we missed him."

"He was at the apartments all day," Kuan Hee said as he placed the van in autonomous mode again, indicating Upper Serangoon Road as destination on the screen.

"So did you find anything suspicious?" Lina said.

"There's nothing secretive in the embassy grounds," Navin said. "Just people going about their work. There doesn't seem to be any covert thing happening."

"Any areas off-limits? Tightly guarded?" Kuan Hee asked.

"Nope. No part of the embassy was out of bounds to us," Tim said. "Nobody bothered about us. We were free to loiter around."

"And no plainclothes guarding the grounds," Navin said. "Just the usual uniformed CISCO guards at the gates."

"That's strange," Kuan Hee said.

"Yeah. We thought it was strange too," Tim said. "We expected them to be hiding things there. It was a disappointment."

"What about you two?" Navin asked.

Lina beat Kuan Hee to the punch. "Loads happening." Like a machinegun, she rattled off in quick succession what they had seen at Cherry Blossoms Apartments, pausing at times to catch her breath. She didn't give Kuan Hee any chance to add his two cents' worth.

Then she sat back in her seat to let the two men in the back digest her stakeout report.

At last, Tim spoke. "Something fishy is going on at the apartments."

"It's all happening in Shelford Road," Navin said, "and not at the Chinese Embassy."

"Same modus operandi as in Medan," Kuan Hee said.

"Let's put everything together, shall we? Kuan Hee said.

"What we do know is they are manufacturing eight human clones," Tim said.

"Two of which they are sending over to Shanghai on Tuesday," Kuan Hee added.

"We don't know for sure where the other clones are going," Navin said. "But I can guess it's also Shanghai."

"We don't know the purpose of these clones," Tim said.

"Or what they look like," Navin said. "Do they look more like robots or human beings?"

"Exactly," Lina said. "Also, can they think like us?"

"Maybe they are only slightly better than robots," Kuan Hee said, "and their AI is only good enough for them to react to situations. They can't reason."

"So many unknowns," Lina said. "Just what is the truth behind these human clones?"

"Beats me," Kuan Hee said.

"May I also add—we don't know who's behind this machination," Tim said.

"So what we need do now," Kuan Hee said, "is to find the answers as quickly as possible. Solve the riddle and put an end to their evil scheme."

"Yeah. Kuan Hee's right," Tim said. "We can't rest till that happens." The other adventurers nodded in unison.

"I suggest we move in two directions," Tim said.

"One—follow the trail of the human clones. Two—track Cao Kun and whom he meets or talks to."

"Good idea," Kuan Hee said.

"I agree," Navin said. "Both directions will eventually meet somewhere along the way and we'll get our answers."

"I'll take care of the human clones," Tim said.

"Then I'll follow Cao Kun," Kuan Hee said, "with Lina."

"I'll partner Tim," Navin said.

"Everything's settled then," Kuan Hee said.

CHAPTER 27

The Brigadier was unassuming as he sat across the table from Kuan Hee and Lina in the ToastBox outlet at the basement level of NEX, a shopping mall in Serangoon Central.

"It's a little warm today," Brigadier Walmsley said as he fanned himself with his hunting hat. "I'm still not used to the tropical heat." Kuan Hee and Lina grinned. The airconditioning had been working extraordinarily well that afternoon.

"Your mother's taking a little longer in Fort Bragg," Brigadier Walmsley said, "because she and your father spent a good few years there. She needs to sort out his things first. You know he's got a lot of research notes she needs to gather." Kuan Hee nodded.

In between sips of his favourite *kopi oh kosong*, the Brigadier regaled Kuan Hee with anecdotes of his adventures in Southeast Asia and finally got to the part about meeting Kuan Hee's father the first time. Then he launched into another long rendition expounding the firm friendship that the two men had forged over the years. Kuan Hee and Lina sat giving attentive ears for the next hour.

The Brigadier was tearing. It was the first time the pair had seen his vulnerable side. He wiped his eyes with a handkerchief.

"Kuan Hee, your father was a noble man," Brigadier Walmsley said. "He had high hopes for his inventions." He paused and then continued. "Alas, he went before his time."

The Brigadier leaned forward and twiddled his thumbs. It was a long minute before he collected his thoughts.

Kuan Hee was anxious to seek the Brigadier's help in putting to practical use his father's mind clone. He could hardly wait longer. But wait he had to, for the Brigadier had started another round.

"You know, Kuan Hee," Brigadier Walmsley said. "Your father believed that we human beings were manufactured by alien beings from a faraway galaxy. That was what got him started in this cloning research. He wanted to replicate the aliens' feat. He wanted to prove this theory—we human beings were clones made by aliens far more advanced than we are."

Without being prompted, the Brigadier had now delved into Kuan Hee's pet question for him. The Brigadier had read his thoughts almost effortlessly. Kuan Hee gazed in amazement.

"Kuan Hee, you are a smart chap," Brigadier Walmsley said. "You take after your father. You should be able to understand what I have just said."

"Yes, Mr Walmsley," Kuan Hee said.

"Fortunately, you father's precious mind clone is safe in your hands," Brigadier Walmsley said. "His life's work is in it. With it, you have the ability to inherit his skills and vast knowledge—instantly." Kuan Hee nodded.

"But, it is a double-edged sword, Kuan Hee," Brigadier Walmsley said. "You gain something precious; you also lose something equally precious."

"Mr Walmsley, that is what I'm curious about," Kuan Hee said. "How do I make use of Dad's mind clone? I don't have the equipment or the expertise."

"That's what I just said, Kuan Hee," Brigadier Walmsley said.

Kuan Hee pondered over what the Brigadier had been rambling about the last few minutes. He stared blankly at the wizened face with the scraggly beard opposite him.

"Kuan Hee, if you are thinking of implanting your father's mind clone in your brain," The Brigadier said, "I'd advise against doing it."

"But, why, Mr Walmsley?" Kuan Hee asked.

"Because—" The Brigadier brought his face close to Kuan Hee's, "—you'll lose your memories once you do it. You will have no knowledge of your past. Everything— Lina, Huei Huei, your friends and your favourite things— will cease to exist in your mind. They will become strangers to you. In their place, new thoughts and feelings, alien to you now, will take over your most intimate spaces." The Brigadier leaned back in his seat.

"Kuan Hee, is that what you want?" Brigadier Walmsley said. "Is it worth sacrificing all that you love?"

"Kuan Hee. It's a horrid idea," Lina lashed out. "You can't do it. You can't forget me. You can't forget Huei Huei. I won't let you." She was almost in tears.

Kuan Hee wrapped his arm across her shoulder. "It's alright. Nothing's happened. We're just talking, that's all."

To inherit all his father's skills and knowledge, Kuan Hee would have to wipe out all his memories. That meant Lina would cease to exist as his beloved. Instead, his mother would be his one and only love. Kuan Hee agonised over this decision he had to make in the coming days.

"Not only will you forget me and Huei Huei. You will even forget your buddies!" Lina said.

"And you won't even remember you want to avenge your father," Brigadier Walmsley said. "So, do you still want to go ahead with it?" He looked at Kuan Hee in the eyes, expecting an answer but receiving none.

"Kuan Hee. Much as I want your father to come alive again," Brigadier Walmsley said. "I can't be selfish and think only of using his knowledge. I have to spare a thought for you. You are his only son—his precious son. I'm sure he'll never want you to take over his mind and lose your own. Not in a million years." The Brigadier paused to take a sip of his coffee. "We'll find another way to sieve his knowledge from his mind clone. Our scientists may be able to do it. It just takes time. Trust us. Trust me, Kuan Hee."

CHAPTER 28

A metallic-silver Mercedes-Benz turned out of the Chinese Embassy gates into the road. Behind its headlamps, a fluttering Chinese stateflag atop a tiny mast announced to one and all the country's top diplomat, the Chinese ambassador, was on an official journey in the back of the limousine.

Two car-lengths behind it, in a rented van, Kuan Hee and Lina kept the limousine in sight.

"Kuan Hee, why are we tailing the ambassador?" Lina asked.

"Cos what the Chinese are doing at Shelford Road setup is just too big for the Chinese ambassador to this country not to know anything about," Kuan Hee said. "He must figure in this somewhere. I can feel it in my bones."

"What if you are wrong?" Lina said.

"Then—it's back to the drawing board," Kuan Hee said. "But, I can bet you I can't be wrong this time round."

The Mercedes-Benz breezed through Orchard Road and entered a service road in front of Paragon, an upper-end mall in the shopping district. It came to a stop in front of the side entrance. Kuan Hee promptly dispatched Little Busy after a stocky balding man in a navy blue business suit who emerged from the back of the limousine.

"Aren't we going to follow him in?" Lina asked.

"It will take time to look for a parking space in this upscale mall," Kuan Hee said. "We can't afford to lose sight of him."

"But I can keep watch on him," Lina insisted.

"Nope. It's not safe for you to do it alone," Kuan Hee said.

The matter settled, Kuan Hee drove the van into the basement car park as Lina watched the Chinese ambassador's movements on the remote's screen.

"The ambassador's entered a bespoke tailor shop on the second level," Lina said.

"OK. Luckily I sent out Little Busy after him. I can't seem to find a vacant lot," Kuan Hee said as he manoeuvred the van around the car park.

"It's Orchard Road, for goodness's sake, Kuan Hee," Lina said. "Everyone comes here to shop."

"Where's the ambassador now?" Kuan Hee asked.

"Still inside," Lina said. "Someone's coming out now. Looks like the ambassador, but dressed differently. He's in an oversized flowery shirt and Bermuda shorts."

Kuan Hee craned his neck to look at the remote's screen. "It's him alright. He's changed out of his office wear. Strange!"

"He's going down the escalator, heading for the taxi stand," Lina said. "He looks grim."

"Gosh! He's leaving the mall," Kuan Hee said. He revved up the van's engine and shot out of the basement car park, oblivious to the honking of several drivers whose right of way he had ignored.

"Where's he now," Kuan Hee asked as he emerged from the car park.

"In a Comfort taxi, moving along Bideford Road towards the Istana," Lina said. "Little Busy's perched itself on the taxi sign."

"Don't tell me he's going to the Istana dressed that

way," Kuan Hee said. Lina shrugged her shoulders in reply.

"The blue taxi in front. That's the one," Lina said.

"Don't worry. I've locked it in my sights now," Kuan Hee said. "We won't lose the ambassador this time."

The Comfort taxi turned left into a road just before the Istana and entered Bukit Timah Road, an arterial road. Then it cruised up the plush residential district.

"He could be heading for Shelford Road," Kuan Hee said.

Just as Kuan Hee had predicted, the blue taxi made a U-turn and glided down the opposite direction, turning into Shelford Road.

"We've hit pay dirt," Kuan Hee said. "He's got to be in the evil scheme too. Cunning devil! Fancy using that switcheroo trick to disguise his tracks."

The taxi unloaded its paying passenger at Cherry Blossoms Apartments and promptly left. Meanwhile, Kuan Hee had parked the van at a shady spot outside. He didn't want the van's metal frame to bake in the searing midday heat; he didn't know how long they would be stationary.

"You guys are in Shelford Road too?" Tim said into his smartphone.

"Yeah," Kuan Hee said into his iPhone. "Whereabouts are you two?"

"On a bench somewhere outside the back gate," Tim said. "We're walking over to you now."

Tim and Navin climbed into the back of the van and settled on some cardboard laid on the floor.

"*Wah!* Nice airconditioning," Navin said as the two men savoured the cool air.

"We were practically melting out there in the sun," Tim complained. "You two are really lucky." Kuan Hee and Lina grinned.

"Seems all directions turn into Shelford Road," Kuan Hee said. "This must be the nerve centre of their operations."

"For sure," Navin said. "Things are getting clearer now. We know the Chinese ambassador figures in this scheme."

"How did you know the ambassador's in it?" Tim asked.

"Lucky hunch, I guess," Kuan Hee said. "Cao Kun's here too?"

Tim nodded. "We have been staking out the place since early morning. Tizzy has its eyes on him right now."

The two insect drones were now perched on different spots in the same place—the conference room. The Chinese ambassador was calling the shots in an armchair at the head of the long table in the room. Around the table sat men and women in lab whites, with Cao Kun on the ambassador's right. Wei Xin was conspicuously absent.

The stocky man roared at his charges. He demanded they quicken their paces. They were behind schedule. Their deadline was drawing near and the people at the top were getting impatient for progress. It was astonishing watching him admonish his audience; they said nary a word.

"What deadline is he talking about?" Kuan Hee asked.

"He didn't say. He merely used *jiézhǐ rìqí* without any elaboration," Lina said.

The adventurers abruptly turned their attention to the meeting, for a sudden loud thud had rung out in the room. The Chinese ambassador had just slammed a pistol on the table. Apparently, he had drawn the weapon he had concealed in his waist.

"What's happening?" Navin asked.

"He's saying if they can't make the deadline, they'll have to face the pistol," Lina said.

"S-e-r-i-o-u-s, man," Tim said.

"I think he means it," Kuan Hee said. "Look at his face. It's fuming red." With the two remotes' screens to watch, the adventurers had two different views of the meeting room; the robot drones had the entire room covered from where they were perched.

"What's Cao Kun saying?" Navin asked.

"He's giving the rundown of the revised schedule for the human clones to leave the lab," Lina said. "Shush! I need to listen."

Just then, the door opened. Wei Xin wheeled himself into the room and stopped on the left of the ambassador. When Cao Kun had finished his presentation, Wei Xin spoke.

"Wei Xin says the first batch of human clones has left safely for Shanghai," Lina said. "He personally saw them off."

The Chinese ambassador broke into loud clapping and the rest of the room followed suit. He was grinning from ear to ear now. It was an abrupt change of mood from earlier on. His pistol was nowhere to be seen on the table.

"What's the schedule?" Kuan Hee asked. Lina referred to her note before replying.

"Total of eight clones to be delivered in four batches. Each batch consists of two clones. Let's see. Delivery of one batch every Thursday starting from today."

"That means—in a month their mission's complete," Kuan Hee said.

"We've got to stop them before then," Tim said. "Before they do more damage."

"Too late to deal with the first batch," Navin said. "It's out of our hands now."

"Shall we tell the Brigadier?" Lina said. "Perhaps, he can help."

"No. Not yet, Lina," Kuan Hee said. "When the time is ripe, perhaps." He wanted to do the crooks in personally; sweet revenge was on his mind. He wasn't going to let anyone or anything stand in his way—not even the Brigadier! It would be better if the Brigadier had no inkling of his selfish plan. But, it was wishful thinking on his part.

"We've got to destroy the human clones en route to the airport," Kuan Hee said. "We don't have the manpower needed to take down this place. There are too many people here. There's also no telling what weapons they've got hidden in the premises. It's too risky to launch an attack here."

"I agree," Tim said. "This place is too big for us four amateurs to handle."

Lina couldn't help but let out a guffaw. The men stared at her in bewilderment.

"The things we've done in the course of our adventures over the years certainly make us much more than amateurs, Tim," Lina explained. "We're virtually experts in the art of spying!" The entire van broke into laughter.

CHAPTER 29

The plan was straightforward. The four adventurers were to waylay the truck conveying the two clones in the vicinity of a fringe road leading to the airport. AleXander the robots with their deadly laser beams and armor-piercing rockets were to figure prominently in the attack plan.

The problem was finding out the truck's route so that the adventurers could lie in wait in a secluded spot. They didn't want to stir up attention by attacking the truck in thick traffic.

"The only way is to tail the truck as it leaves Cherry Blossom Apartments," Tim said. "But, we may be discovered before we can make our move."

"It's a risk we have to take," Kuan Hee said.

"Why can't we attack the truck outside the apartments, say along Shelford Road?" Lina asked.

"Cos then they will know their lab's secret location has been exposed. They will move elsewhere," Tim said, "and we'll never be able to find them again."

"Then we strike them in one fell swoop at the apartments," Lina said.

"Gosh! Lina, you think too highly of us and our abilities," Navin said.

"We'll be dead meat before we get near the clones, Lina," Tim said.

"Lina, this is a big group we're up against," Kuan Hee said. "It's not like our previous adventures."

"Kuan Hee is right," Tim said. "So a surprise attack is the best choice."

"Correction. It's the only choice," Navin said.

Next Thursday morning found Navin and Lina staking out Cherry Blossoms Apartments from behind a bush along Shelford Road. They let Little Busy fly into the compound to look for the truck, which would deliver the two clones to the airfreight multiplex at Terminal 5 in Changi Airport.

It seemed the two adventurers were too early. The truck was parked in the front porch, but its back doors were wide open. There was nothing inside. But the compound was abuzz with activity. In the driveway, there were men with menacing looks lingering around two cars. At the front porch, men in lab whites were hauling large boxes out of the front entrance. Soon, they were loading these into the truck. Wei Xin appeared at the front door. He barked orders to the men in lab whites. Little Busy hovered in the air near the walls of the building.

"I don't see human clones anywhere, do you?" Navin said.

"Don't tell me they are in the boxes," Lina said.

"One. Two. Three. Four. I count four boxes," Navin said. "Three in the truck and one on the porch."

"Two of the boxes are large enough to hold an adult in a sitting position," Lina said. "They've got 'Diplomatic Bag' stickers on them."

"Yeah. The clones could be in them," Navin said. "There's nothing else going into the truck."

"They're shutting the doors," Lina said. "We must be right."

"Quick! Get Little Busy on top of the truck," Navin

said.

Lina let Little Busy fly over the truck and attach itself to the top of the driver's cabin.

"Little Busy's in position," Lina said. "I'll WhatsApp Kuan Hee to let him know." She started tapping on her Samsung smartphone.

"Now. We wait," Navin said. "I think the two cars are going together with the truck."

"I'll turn Little Busy's cameras on them," Lina said.

They saw two men helping Wei Xin into one of the cars. Then all the men boarded the vehicles and the convoy of three vehicles rolled out of the driveway into Shelford Road.

"Wei Xin's in the first car with two men," Navin said. "Another two men in the driver's cabin of the truck and two more in the car behind."

"OK. I'm sending the info to Kuan Hee right now," Lina said.

The vehicles moved past the hidden adventurers and disappeared into a bend in the road.

"There's nothing more we can do here," Navin said. "Let's go. It's going to be a long walk to the main road from here." They patted the grass off their clothes and trod down the road. Lina kept her eyes on the remote's screen. She needed to update Kuan Hee on the route taken by the convoy.

Meanwhile, Kuan Hee and Tim had parked the van along Tanah Merah Coast Road, just before it forked into Changi East Drive. The two men started their long wait for the truck to travel from the middle of the island to the east coast.

"Don't turn off the engine," Tim said. "It's a hot day. I don't want to melt in the van."

"The truck is moving along the Pan Island Expressway," Kuan Hee said, looking at Lina's WhatsApp message on his iPhone.

Tim brought up a map of the island and zoomed in on

the Pan Island Expressway. He fingered the roads in Changi East, which the Pan Island Expressway connected to. "The logical choice would be for the truck to turn right into East Coast Parkway after the Pan Island Expressway. From there, it will do two left turns, first into Tanah Merah Coast Road and then into Changi East Drive. Thereafter, it'll turn left again into the Cargo Terminal Megaplex, where the airfreight terminal is located."

"I think so too," Kuan Hee said. "We're here, at the junction of Tanah Merah Coast Road and Changi East Drive. The truck has to pass us to get to the airfreight megaplex in Terminal 5. We'll ambush it here." He took AleXander the robots out of his backpack. They stood with their arms at their sides, as if ready to move off at a moment's notice. Kuan Hee pressed a button on the robots' back and their front panels flipped open. Both robots were now armed and primed for action.

Kuan Hee's iPhone chimed again. It was Lina on WhatsApp. The convoy had turned into East Coast Parkway. It was only minutes away from Kuan Hee and Tim.

Kuan Hee got down from the driver's seat and climbed into the back of the van while Tim slid over to take the wheel.

"We don't have any hardware with us," Tim said. "So we have to be extra careful."

"Don't worry, I'll keep Alex by our side. Its laser beams will protect us," Kuan Hee said. "Xander will work his rockets on our target."

At Kuan Hee's command, Xander leapt out of the van and stood with its feet apart about a metre into the road, ready to pounce on its unsuspecting victims who would be coming up on the road behind them. The robot was only thirty centimetres tall; no one would notice it.

By now, the convoy had turned into Changi East Drive. Kuan Hee could see the vehicles from the back window of the van. Little Busy had already lifted itself into the air and flown to safety. It was time for Xander to do its work.

"I'll let the first car pass," Kuan Hee told Tim. He dragged the glass window open and waited for the precise moment before shouting some commands to Xander.

At once, Xander leapt into the path of the truck and launched two rockets successively from its arsenal. Though tiny, the rockets packed a punch. Each one could blast a hole through an army tank. The rockets hit the truck, sending it up in smoke in seconds. It was now a burning heap of metal. The car behind the truck could not stop in time to avoid a collision. It exploded into flames instantly.

By now, Xander had jumped into the van, which roared away from the burning wreckage. From the back window, Kuan Hee saw the lead car in the convoy stop in the middle of the road. Two men were helping Wei Xin out of the car. Wei Xin was gesticulating frantically. He was hopping mad.

Kuan Hee allowed a wicked smile to betray his abhorrence of the scene of carnage behind him.

"It's a piece of cake," Tim declared. Kuan Hee could not agree more.

"I could have sent Wei Xin up in flames too," Kuan Hee said. But he didn't. Say what he would, Kuan Hee didn't have the heart to set Wei Xin ablaze, for doing so was akin to destroying his father, whose mind had been installed in the evil scientist's brain.

CHAPTER 30

That evening, the four adventurers sat in the living room of 79 Jalan Nuang, pondering their next move.

"The Chinese aren't going to take this lying down," Tim said. "We've struck at their heart. They will hit back—and hard. We've got to be ready for the backlash when it comes."

"But we have an advantage," Kuan Hee said. "I don't think they know who hit them yet. By the time they do, we'll have destroyed the rest of the human clones."

"Too bad I wasn't there when Xander launched his rockets," Navin said. "I bet it was fun."

"The flames shot up a few storeys high," Tim said.

"Wei Xin's jaw practically dropped open," Kuan Hee added.

"But people died you know," Lina said.

"They deserved it," Kuan Hee said. "Doing evil doesn't pay."

"Couldn't we have just destroyed the clones without killing the men in the truck too?" Lina said.

"If the truck had reached the cargo megaplex, it would have been too late to stop it," Kuan Hee said. "Lina, these people's heinous plot—if successful, could put many more people's lives in danger. Besides, the men in the truck looked like thugs. At the very least, we had stopped them doing more evil. Goodness knows how many people they have killed in their lives."

"Let's not dwell on it," Tim said. "What's done is done."

"Yeah. We've got to figure out how to deal with the next batch of human clones," Navin said. "I don't think these guys will use the same route to the airport."

"I vote we stake out Shelford Road again," Tim said. "Find out their plans."

"Won't they be on the alert?" Lina said. "It'll be dangerous getting so near to them."

"We have no choice, Lina," Kuan Hee said. "Perhaps, you should stay out of the next mission."

Without a word, Lina stormed out of the room. Then she returned and glared at him. "I'll do no such thing. You're horrid, Kuan Hee."

"Pipe down, guys," Tim said.

"Look! The burning inferno's on TV," Navin said.

The adventurers' attention turned to the large wall-mounted television set in front of them. The seven o'clock news was airing and a female news presenter was shown, on site, reporting the incident. They heard her saying that four charred bodies—beyond recognition—had been dragged out of the debris. A representative of the Chinese Embassy appeared on the news clip telling the presenter the embassy's truck had been en route to the airport when it suddenly exploded. When asked for a possible reason, he replied he was clueless.

"They are covering up the incident," Tim said.

"For obvious reasons, they want to keep it under wraps," Kuan Hee said.

"Wei Xin's nowhere in sight," Kuan Hee said.

"It's a secretive project," Navin said. "I'm sure they don't want him showing his face on national TV."

"I still can't figure out why he's in a wheelchair," Kuan

Hee said. "It is one of two burning questions in my mind."

"So what's the other, Kuan Hee?" Navin asked.

"Huh?" Kuan Hee said. "Oh! How should I put it? I don't know how he managed to control my dad's mind in him. I mean, my dad's mind went into his brain right? So his own mind should have been wiped out. So how is it he's still in control of his own mind?"

"You're not making sense, Kuan Hee," Lina said.

Tim came to Kuan Hee's rescue. "Remember Jordan? His father erased his memories and installed his own memories in Jordan's brain. Look what happened then. Jordan wasn't himself. He couldn't recognize us. He had become his father."

"What Kuan Hee wants to say is Wei Xin shouldn't remember who he really is—but he does," Navin said.

"Kinda complicated, isn't it?" Lina said.

"I guess so," Kuan Hee said. "In Jordan's case, there was a Jekyll and Hyde moment. Sometimes, Jordan would wake up and assume control of his own mind. Other times, his father reigned in his mind. So I thought in Wei Xin's case, things would pretty much be the same. But they aren't. That's the problem. I just can't figure out why it's different this time and how the Chinese scientists managed to let Wei Xin control his own mind—not let my dad's mind take over totally."

"Amazing. Simply amazing," Tim said. "The Chinese must have some pretty talented people in their payroll."

"Of course they do," Navin said. "With a population of nearly two billion people, finding talented people should be a breeze."

"We are Chinese too," Lina said. "We Chinese are good at science and technology."

"And we Indians are good at mathematics and computer programming," Navin added.

"Guys. Stop typecasting our races," Tim said. He was the voice of reason in their group. "Don't generalize our talents into the moulds you think they fit. Talented people exist everywhere—in every race."

"Tim's right," Kuan Hee said. "We shouldn't be sterotyping people. It's mean."

"OK. OK," Navin said. "Now, where were we? How did we get sidetracked?"

"Beats me," Kuan Hee said.

"So what were we talking about?" Tim asked.

"Kuan Hee's two burning questions," Lina said.

"Oh. Yes. My two burning questions," Kuan Hee parroted. "I wonder—the reason Wei Xin's in a wheelchair. Maybe the operation on him went awry. That's the only plausible explanation I've been able to come up with."

"Wah! Even with these scientists' brilliant minds, things can go wrong," Lina said. "Kuan Hee. Your father must be the best scientist around." Kuan Hee smiled. "No, *lah*."

"That's humility for you," Navin said.

"Plain flattering to me," Tim said. "Wife buttering up husband." Everyone broke into laughter. The mood in the room had lightened up.

"But, the Chinese scientists must have found a way to inhibit certain portions of my dad's mind," Kuan Hee said, "so that Wei Xin still has some control over his mind. This explains why Wei Xin didn't come looking for me and Mum. My Dad's mind isn't in control. Wei Xin's not my Dad."

"Kuan Hee, you were telling us you want to install your father's mind in yours," Tim said. "Is that for real?"

"He's not going to do it," Lina said. "Not ever—if I can help it."

"I was just exploring the idea," Kuan Hee said. "But, I don't think I can go far. I can't even make a copy of my own mind. The whole process is beyond me. I'll need my dad's—the Brigadier's research team. It's not even a possibility."

"Thank heavens for that," Lina said.

"Kuan Hee, did you speak to the Brigadier about it?"

Tim asked.

"I sure did," Kuan Hee said, "when Lina and I met him at NEX recently."

"So did he warm up to your idea?" Navin asked.

"On the contrary, he kept trying to talk Kuan Hee out of it," Lina said.

"No. He didn't," Kuan Hee said.

"He did," Lina said. "I should know. I was sitting beside you when he lectured you on the dangers of mind cloning."

"What exactly did the Brigadier say, Kuan Hee?" Tim asked.

"The Brigadier told me that human cloning is outlawed by the United Nations. It prohibits all forms of human cloning. He went on to say everyone's doing it, turning a blind eye to the law in the interest of science. Cos the lure of making a real live human clone in our lifetime is simply irresistible."

"I remember the Brigadier advised you against it," Lina said. "I distinctly remember him asking you whether it was worth sacrificing everything you love for it." Kuan Hee was silent for the next few minutes. Lina had hit paydirt with her words. The other adventurers looked at each other, not knowing what to say.

It was Tim who broke the uneasy silence in the room. "Maybe, in time, you will learn how to do it. Then you can harness his skills and knowledge. It won't be too late."

"Yes. Tim's right," Navin said. "You can wait, can't you? You are still young. We're all still young."

"Perhaps, you guys are right," Kuan Hee said. "Perhaps, I was a little rash. I should be glad my dad lives on in the 3D images etched in the holographic optical data storage drive." He paused. "What matters is—this data storage drive is safe in my hands. Nothing else matters."

"Yeah. Kuan Hee, nothing else matters," Lina echoed.

"What's our next move?" Navin asked. He was eager to move on with the discussion.

"Guess we continue to stakeout Shelford Road," Tim said. "It's the only way to keep abreast of their development."

"Not so," Navin said. "Remember the Chinese Embassy?"

"Oh yeah. I forgot," Tim said.

"For sure, they will make changes to their schedule," Kuan Hee said.

"Why not you and Lina keep tabs on Cao Kun and the Chinese ambassador? Navin and I will keep an eye on Shelford Road," Tim said. The adventurers nodded in unison.

CHAPTER 31

The Chinese Embassy in Tanglin Road was crawling with plainclothes when Kuan Hee and Lina arrived for a day of reconnaissance in their rental van. Except for their civilian attire, the plainclothes looked like they belonged to a uniformed corp.

"Must be Chinese agents," Kuan Hee said. After releasing Little Busy into the air, he drove the van away from the embassy, parking it along the road a hundred metres away from the embassy gates. "It's safer here."

Little Busy busied itself following the ambassador as he went about his business. The ambassador was in a bad mood today, ranting and raving as he negotiated the corridors of the embassy with his minders at his heels.

"What's he complaining about?" Kuan Hee asked.

"I can't hear him clearly," Lina said. "Let me get Little Busy nearer to him." At her direction, Little Busy sped after the ambassador. It was now hovering above him.

A minder came up to the ambassador with news of the arrival of visitors from Beijing. They were waiting for him in his office.

"The ambassador is rushing to his office," Kuan Hee said. "Must be important visitors. Let's see who they are."

Flitting into a large room at a secluded corner of the ground floor, Little Busy saw two visitors rising from a sofa to shake hands with the ambassador. All three sat down to conversation. The ambassador's minders had excused themselves from the room.

"The visitors are from the Central Government Investigative Unit in Beijing," Lina said. "They are here to probe the case of the burning truck. The older man is Zhang He Jun and the other Wang Chen Ming."

"They do work fas—"

"Shush!" Lina said. "Let me hear them talk first."

The minutes passed. To Kuan Hee, these were agonizing minutes. He longed to hear what Lina had to tell him about the men's conversation.

"Lina, just what are they saying?" Kuan Hee asked.

"It's strange. They aren't talking about the human clones," Lina said. "Instead, the ambassador is telling them a short circuit in the electrical wiring of the truck caused it to go up in flames. He deeply regretted the loss of four lives."

"*Wah seh*," Kuan Hee said. "Why is the ambassador hiding the truth? These visitors are not in cahoots with the ambassador after all."

"The four dead men are from the Military Attache Office," Lina said. "The investigators are asking what they were escorting to the airport."

"So what did the ambassador tell them?" Kuan Hee asked.

"He claims he needs clearance from Beijing to release the info to them," Lina said. "But these men are from Beijing. I'm confused."

"I think he's playing for time," Kuan Hee said. "The investigators' visit must have taken him by surprise."

"If the Chinese government has sanctioned the human clones, why does he need to hide things from them?" Lina asked.

"Search me," Kuan Hee said. "Could be these

investigators have not been cleared to receive top-secret info. The human clones are a top-secret project."

After the investigators from Beijing had left the room, Cao Kun came in, shoulders hunched. Something had cowed him into reticence. This time, when he spoke, it was in a subdued tone. But he didn't get a chance to say much, for the ambassador was in a fiery mood, waving his hands in the air as he reprimanded the man.

"Their plan is in disarray. They need time to manufacture replacement clones. The ambassador says their master is furious," Lina said.

"Master? They have a master?"

"*Zhǔzi*. That's what the ambassador said," Lina said. "It means 'master'."

"Lina, every word they say is important," Kuan Hee said. "Don't miss a single word."

"Don't worry. I won't," Lina said. She was glad her mastery of Chinese was proving useful to Kuan Hee. She was a valuable asset to him after all.

"*Alamak!* We forgot to tail the investigators," Kuan Hee said.

"But, we only have Little Busy with us," Lina said. "Tizzy is with Tim and Navin."

Meanwhile, on a grassy verge outside the back gate of Cherry Blossoms Apartments in Shelford Road, Tim and Navin sat. Tim was fiddling with his iPad while Navin kept his eyes glued on Tizzy's remote control. Tizzy was on duty in the apartments' compound, taking in the activities of the Chinese operatives. It had to be careful not to be spotted today, for there were two drones hovering over the premises. Plainclothes were milling around in the compound. The Chinese were taking no chances.

"Are these drones able to sense Tizzy's presence?" Navin asked.

"I really don't know," Tim said. "The drones are unlike those we see in the shops. They could be used for military surveillance. They might be able to sense heat from the equipment in Tizzy's body. Just keep Tizzy away from them."

"Don't worr—"

There was a commotion where the two adventurers sat. Someone had come up behind Navin and wrapped him in his arms. Navin let out a cry, but it was too late. He passed out from a knock on the nape of his head. Tim wriggled out of the strong arms of another man. He staggered to his feet and made for the bushes below, with the man barely metres behind him. Suddenly a shot rang out. Tim fell and rolled down the slope. The man who fired the shot stumbled down the slope after him. At the bottom of the slope, Tim heaved himself up and wobbled towards the busy Bukit Timah junction. His first thoughts were to get to where people were clustered. He was oblivious to the intense pain radiating down his back. *The hawker centre— must reach the hawker centre.* In the car park outside the hawker centre, he collapsed. Quickly, people milled around him. Someone stooped to lend a helping hand, while another pressed some tissue paper on his bleeding back. A third called for an ambulance.

Back in the van parked along Tanglin Road, Kuan Hee and Lina had no inkling of the drama unfolding behind Shelford Road.

"Tim is not updating the WhatsApp group chat," Lina said. "Navin's not answering either."

"Keep trying," Kuan Hee said. "Maybe, it's a network problem."

But the minutes passed uneventfully. Both Tim's and Navin's smartphones were not responding to their calls. Kuan Hee feared the worst.

"Quick! We've got to go to Shelford Road," Kuan Hee said. He revved the van's engine and it roared to life. It sped off towards the Chinese Embassy. The pair had to pick up Little Busy first. With the robot drone safely on board, the van raced towards the plush Bukit Timah district.

The mood was somber in the van. Silence prevailed the entire journey. Soon the van reached Lornie Road, which faced the back of the Shelford Road residences. Kuan Hee stopped the van along the road and, leaving a reluctant Lina behind in the van, clambered up the grassy slope to where Tim and Navin were supposed to position themselves. There was no one in sight. He scanned the grassy verge. The grass was flattened at one spot. *Tim and Navin had to be sitting here.* Kuan Hee moved around the spot, kicking the grass as he hovered over it. There was nothing lying in it. Tim and Navin were nowhere to be seen. So were their backpacks and Tizzy's remote control. *Where have they gone?* He looked down the slope, trying to find clues. Then he retraced his steps to the main road below. Near the bottom of the slope, he saw what looked like bloodstains on the grass. He knelt beside the stains for a close look. *It's blood all right.* At once, he felt a shiver down his spine. *Something has happened to them.* He ran back to the van.

"Kuan Hee, look—across the road," Lina screeched.

Kuan Hee turned his eyes to the car park across the road. There were scores of people—under trees, on pavements, among parked cars—everywhere. Something had happened.

"Wait here. Don't you dare move," Kuan Hee shouted. He dashed across the road to where the crowd had gathered. He elbowed his way through the throng of people, to the focus of attention. There, lying limp in a man's arms was—Tim! Kuan Hee dropped to his knees and cradled his bosom friend in his arms.

"I'm here, Tim," Kuan Hee said. "Hang on, dear friend."

"We're waiting for the ambulance," the man who had been holding Tim said. "Are you his friend?" Kuan Hee nodded. He was tearing. He took a wad of tissue paper from his pocket and pressed it on Tim's back.

"The ambulance's taking ages to arrive," Kuan Hee complained. Tim was delirious. He was mumbling away.

Finally, the ambulance pulled into the car park. Attendants packed Tim into the ambulance and, sirens wailing, the ambulance sped into the traffic. But not before Kuan Hee found out where it was taking Tim.

Kuan Hee sprinted back to the van across the road. On seeing his bloodied hands and shirt, Lina screamed. He folded her in his arms and comforted her. She was too squeamish to handle traumatic situations. It was minutes before her cries petered out. It was time to rush to Tan Tock Seng Hospital, where Tim had been taken.

At the Accidents & Emergency department of Tan Tock Seng Hospital, the pair loitered, waiting for news of Tim. It was to be a long wait. Tim had been rolled into an operating theatre. Doctors were now operating on him.

Images of the day's happenings flitted past Kuan Hee's mind as he sat slumped in a chair beside Lina. *I should have been more careful. I'm to blame.* His thoughts wandered to Navin. He sat up suddenly. *Navin's been caught.* He scanned his iPhone for messages and missed calls; there were none. *Navin must be in their hands.* Fear gripped his consciousness. He lingered in a state of shock. *What can I do? What must I do?*

Kuan Hee's best pals Tim and Navin were in trouble. He had no one to turn to. Lina was no help in this chaotic situation. The least he could do was to keep her calm. He had to compose himself or he risked getting her going emotional again. *I must rescue Navin. They'll torture him for sure. I must get to him before it's too late.* He never felt more helpless.

"Tim is safe now," Kuan Hee said. "The doctors are attending to him." He was trying to pacify Lina.

"Lina, you stay here. Wait for news," Kuan Hee said. "I need to go look for Navin."

"No! Kuan Hee. No! It's too dangerous," Lina

squealed. "You can't go alone. You could be killed."

But Kuan Hee's mind was set. He was adamant to save Navin no matter what he took—even if he had to die, he would not have any second thoughts. He pulled her away from him. "Listen, Lina. Pull yourself together, for goodness's sake. I—we can't very well let Navin die. I've got to save him. You look after Tim here. I'll be back soon. Trust me." Not looking back, Kuan Hee tore off through the hall, heading for the van in the basement, leaving behind a wailful Lina.

CHAPTER 32

As the van raced through the suburban district towards Bukit Timah, Kuan Hee's thoughts were on Navin. *He must be alive. He's got to be somewhere in Cherry Blossoms Apartments. I'll find him if it's the last thing I get to do.* The minutes fleeted past. Kuan Hee didn't know where Tim had hidden the SAR21s. The rifles, which hadn't been used in the past three years, had to be in deep storage in Tim's father's warehouse in Paya Lebar. Kuan Hee had to mount the rescue without them. He inhaled deeply. He had arrived outside the apartments in Shelford Road. It was time for action. Kuan Hee let Alex and Xander out of his backpack. They were his weapons. They would protect him from harm; they would help him rescue Navin safely.

Leaving the van by the roadside, Kuan Hee stole along the perimeter wall of the apartments, with the two robots at his heels. He set Little Busy into the air over the wall and watched the drone housefly broadcast live images of the compound on the remote's screen. Little Busy's work wasn't as easy as before. Now it had to hide from the two drones circling the air over the compound.

There was no time to lose. Kuan Hee had to find Navin quickly. There was no telling what these evil men would do to his best pal.

Little Busy flitted into the long building and explored the corridors on the upper floor. It entered the laboratory easily, for men and women in lab whites, wearing anxious looks, were scurrying around. But there was no sign of Navin. There was a line of gurneys with people lying on them in a corner of the laboratory. Kuan Hee piloted the robot housefly over them. At first look, the people on the gurneys were unfamiliar middle-aged Chinese men to him. They appeared to be asleep. Then one face stood out from the rest. There was a hint of recognition in Kuan Hee's eyes. He paused Little Busy over the figure. Kuan Hee's face lit up. The figure had the unmistakable broad cheeks. It was the Chinese President! Or was it? *Oh no. It's a clone of the President! Gosh! It so resembles the President. There's no way to tell them apart.* There was a moment of silence as Kuan Hee took in the full impact of his discovery. *Horror of Horrors! These evil men intend to usurp power. They are using human clones to take over the Chinese government!* Kuan Hee sank against the perimeter wall. *I was wrong. It's not the Chinese government that's stealing Dad's secrets. It's someone or some group that's intent on replacing China's top leaders with lookalike human clones. I've got to stop them before they can do harm.*

Kuan Hee knew he had to make a decision. Carry on looking for Navin or destroy the human clones. He could only do one. He was sure Navin wasn't on the upper floor, so he barked orders to Alex and Xander. All three climbed over the wall. Once they landed on the ground inside the compound, Kuan Hee threw all caution to the wind. The three intruders sprinted to the end of the building and entered a door. Then they climbed the stairs to the upper floor and stopped at the double-leaved glass doors. At Kuan Hee's command, Alex the robot burned a hole through the lock on the door. Kuan Hee opened the door and all three ran through the laboratory to the astonishment of the men and women in lab whites who tried to stop them. Seeing the gurneys ahead of them,

Kuan Hee uttered a string of orders to Alex. At once, the robot directed a stream of laser beams at its target. The first few gurneys lit up in flames. Before Alex could shoot another volley of laser beams, some men had grabbed hold of the remaining two gurneys and whisked them out of firing range of Alex's laser weapons system.

Shots rang out in the laboratory. Men were shooting at Kuan Hee. He threw himself onto the ground, narrowly escaping a bullet. At his insruction, Xander the robot leapt onto a table and launched a rocket at their attackers. A loud boom rang out. Windows shattered and body parts splattered across the room. Xander's rocket was menacingly powerful. Ahead of the intruders was a mangled mess of metal and human flesh. Fire had broken out in the laboratory. The intense heat activated fire sprinklers on the ceiling. In seconds, sprinkers were spraying copious amounts of water all over the laboratory, causing the floor to be flooded.

Kuan Hee picked himself up. In the chaos, he and his robots made their escape through a window, leaping one floor onto the grassy patch behind the building. He sprained his ankle on impact with the ground. Alex and Xander, being virtually indestructible, landed without incident. He limped towards the back gate with Alex and Xander flanking him. There, a guard raised his gun at the trio. Alex stopped him in his tracks. Its laser beams reduced him to a smouldering heap at Kuan Hee's order. Such was the price of incurring Kuan Hee's wrath, which knew no bounds when stoked. It was a simple task for Alex to break open the back gate. Without once looking back, the party of three fled the scene.

CHAPTER 33

After his successful operation to remove a bullet lodged in his back, Tim spent the next four hours under observation in a ward next to the operating theatre, out of sight of visitors.

Lina was leaning on the back of a chair, eyes closed, in the wide corridor outside the operating theatre when Kuan Hee came up to her and pecked her forehead. She opened her weary eyes. Glad to see Kuan Hee safe and sound, she lurched forward and grabbed his waist, sobbing into his shirt. He patted her back.

"How's Tim?" Kuan Hee asked.

"He hasn't woken up yet. He's in a room over there," Lina said, pointing to one end of the corridor, "waiting for the anaesthetic drug to wear off. The doctor says he'll be fine."

Kuan Hee sat next to Lina. "Where's Navin? Did you find him?" She asked.

Kuan Hee brought clasped hands over the back of his head and rested them against it. "I didn't manage to find him. They had hidden him somewhere else. But, I did manage to destroy some of the human clones."

"Where can they have hidden Navin?" Lina asked.

Kuan Hee shook his head. "I have no idea. I really have no idea. I'll try looking for him tomorrow. The embassy should hold some clues."

The windows at the end of the corridor began to darken. Soon it was brighter in the corridor than outside the window, which turned black in the dwindling light. Slowly, tiny lights of different hues of the rainbow sprouted all over the window. The night cityscape had come alive as a kaleidoscope of colours outside the windows.

Visiting hours had ended. But for Kuan Hee and Lina, it marked the start of their ward visit; Tim had just been wheeled into a four-bedded ward on the second level.

Tim forced a weak smile to peek out of his face. He tried to sit up, but Kuan Hee wouldn't allow it. Kuan Hee placed another pillow below Tim's head to prop it up.

"I say, you're looking good," Kuan Hee said. "Better than I looked when I was lying there three years ago."

"Aw, Kuan Hee," Lina said. "Don't tease him."

"I'm sorry Navin got taken," Tim said. "I was too careless."

"It's over, Tim," Kuan Hee said. "It's not your fault. These men are professionals. We can't beat them at their game."

"Do you know where they have taken him?" Tim asked.

Kuan Hee shrugged his shoulders in reply. "I didn't find Navin at Cherry Blossoms Apartments, but I got wind of the Chinese ambassador's heinous plot," Kuan Hee said.

"Heinous plot?" Tim repeated. "What heinous plot?"

"In the laboratory, on one of the gurneys lay a human clone with remarkable resemblance to the Chinese President."

"He looks like him?" Tim said.

"To a T," Kuan Hee said. "It's my deduction that these evil men have hatched a plot to take over the legitimate

Chinese leadership. They plan to usurp power."

"The Chinese President is on par with the United States President," Lina said. "If they succeed, they will control half the world."

"Precisely," Kuan Hee said. "We've destroyed four clones. They are left with four, including the Chinese President lookalike."

"But they still have the most powerful clone with them," Tim said. "They can do a great deal of damage with just that one."

"So I have to find out where they have hidden the Chinese President lookalike," Kuan Hee. "I won't rest till I do."

"How will you do that?" Tim asked.

"By shadowing Wei Xin," Kuan Hee said. "I have a strong feeling he will lead me to the clones. But, I will also go looking for Navin again—first thing tomorrow. I promise."

"Don't worry, Tim," Lina said in a tremulous voice. "Kuan Hee will bring Navin back. We'll be all together again—for sure."

CHAPTER 34

The next morning found Kuan Hee fiddling with his iPhone. He had spent a good hour downloading an app and testing it on his iPhone. Looking pleased with himself, he settled down for breakfast with Lina.

"I've found a way to understand what the Chinese are saying without you as a go-between," Kuan Hee said, raising his iPhone in the air. "See? This app is the answer. It provides translation on the fly. We'll use it afterwards."

"You mean, you don't need me anymore?" Lina lamented.

"No. Lina, not like that," Kuan Hee explained. "It's just that you won't need to waste time translating for me. The app will do it as it hears the person talk. It will free you for more important things."

"More important things?" Lina's face lit up. She was no longer cross. Kuan Hee heaved a sigh of relief. It wasn't easy for him living with Lina's temperamental nature.

"I'm leaving for the Chinese Embassy," Kuan Hee said.

"I'm coming with you," Lina said.

"But it's dangerous," Kuan Hee said. "Look at what happened to Tim and Navin. I don't want anything happening to you."

"Take me along, Kuan Hee," Lina said. "I promise I won't be in the way. I'll listen to you."

At the Chinese Embassy, the ambassador was in conference with his lieutenants. Listening in on the conversation from his van parked half a street away, Kuan Hee delighted in his success with the new app he had downloaded into his iPhone. The translation was almost seamless.

"It might be impossible to salvage the situation. Li ZhanNan is flying into town tomorrow morning," the Chinese ambassador said. "We've to be ready with answers, or our heads will roll." At once, his audience stood up and bowed their heads low.

Next to speak was Wei Xin. He assured the ambassador that nothing would happen to the remaining two human clones in his custody. "The two clones will leave for Shanghai the next morning. I'll personally accompany them."

"So will I," Cao Kun said.

"The young man you caught outside the apartments," the ambassador said. "Have you gotten anything out of him?" Kuan Hee and Lina cocked their ears. Kuan Hee brought his iPhone closer to them.

"He's a stubborn guy," Cao Kun said. "Give me a few more days. I'll have him eating out of my hand."

"Remember, I don't want him dead—yet," the ambassador said. "I want to find out who are behind this scheme to destroy our human clones. I want them to pay dearly for what they have done."

"Rest assured, I'll get him talking," Cao Kun said.

"So Cao Kun's the one holding Navin captive," Kuan Hee said. "Follow him and we'll find out Navin's whereabouts."

"Who are we following? Wei Xin or Cao Kun?" Lina said. "We can't follow both of them. We don't have the manpower." Kuan Hee scratched his head, trying to think of a solution, but found none.

"Look! Wei Xin's leaving the meeting," Lina said.

"He could be going back to his office," Kuan Hee said. But he didn't. He wheeled himself out of the building to a waiting van. There, two men pushed him up a ramp into the vehicle, which moved out of the embassy with all three on board and Little Busy clinging on the roof above the windshield.

"Aren't you going to tail Cao Kun?" Lina said. "He knows where Navin is."

"But we've got to find the human clones before they leave Singapore," Kuan Hee said as he kept Wei Xin's van in sight.

"Isn't Navin more important than those clones?" Lina said. "He's our good friend. We can't leave him in the lurch."

"I won't. I promise," Kuan Hee said. "The clones are leaving tomorrow. Once they leave, we are powerless to stop them. Navin can wait a little while. Didn't you hear the ambassador? They won't do anything to him yet."

"I can't believe you, Kuan Hee," Lina said. "Is revenge that important to you? More important than your best friend?"

"Lina, we've got to see the big picture," Kuan Hee said. "We've got to rid the world of these human clones— before they can do damage."

"Kuan Hee, you have changed. You are blinded by revenge," Lina said.

Knowing it was pointless to continue the debate with Kuan Hee, Lina did the only thing she could—she sulked.

CHAPTER 35

The two vans cruised along the traffic-heavy expressways in the heart of Singapore. Kuan Hee was careful to keep three car-lengths behind Wei Xin's van. *Nothing must spoil my plan to destroy the clones.*

The vans filtered into a sub-urban road. At a junction stop, Kuan Hee grabbed Alex and Xander the robots. He punched a button on their back and a panel on their chest opened. They were now primed for firing.

The two vans resumed their journey eastwards towards Upper Changi Road and then Simei Avenue, where they turned into an industrial park.

"They are not using a house this time," Kuan Hee said. But Lina was not listening.

The first van entered a gate and came to a halt in front of an old single-storeyed concrete building with a flat roof and casement windows. There was a man behind a small desk outside the front door. He rose to greet the visitors.

Little Busy lifted itself into the air and surveyed the premises. Used vehicle parts lined one end wall. The entire place looked more like a workshop than a sophisticated laboratory. Its neighbours were grimy workshops dealing with car repairs and auto spare parts. Loud knocking sounds pierced the air intermittently in the neighbourhood.

Kuan Hee and Lina sat in the van, which he had parked diagonally opposite the building. He turned up the volume on Little Busy's remote and his iPhone. The clanging of metal in the workshops around them made listening to conversations difficult. Luckily, the translation app had no difficulty picking up the conversation.

"This place is too noisy for work," a man said. "It's also dirty and greasy."

"I couldn't come up with anything better at short notice," Wei Xin said. "Just bear with it. Make do with what you have. Anyway, we'll be leaving here tomorrow."

"Is the equipment packed and ready?" Wei Xin asked.

"Almost done," the man said, pointing to a row of crates on one side of the workspace. "What about the rest of the stuff in Shelford Road?"

"Leave them there," Wei Xin said. "I'll be able to get another place ready by next week. You can move them then." He wheeled himself to the back of the building. "Let's take a look at the clones."

In a large air-conditioned room, three men in lab whites were at work—one in front of a computer, and the other two connecting wires to two figures on gurneys.

"How are the memory tests?" Wei Xin asked.

"The scans indicate their brain waves are regular," one of the men in lab whites said. "The explosion has done no damage to them. But we need another twenty-four hours before we can give an all clear."

"We can't wait," Wei Xin said. "The flight is at 9:00 a.m. You can continue your tests when we arrive in Shanghai. The master is getting impatient."

"Lina, wait here," Kuan Hee said, getting down from the van. "I'm going inside the building." Lina grudgingly obliged. She still wasn't talking to him.

"Alex and Xander, heel," Kuan Hee said. It was the command for them to stay at his side.

All three sidled up to the building on their left.

"Kuan Hee!" Lina screamed. Before Kuan Hee could react, a man had come up behind him and wrapped him in his arms. Another man placed a hand across his mouth, preventing him from making any sound. They took him into the compound. A third man emerged from the front gate, looking for Lina. Instinctively, she locked herself in the van and crammed her petite body into the small space below the dashboard. She was shivering with fear—not just for her safety but also for Kuan Hee's. She did not expect things to turn up this way, not when she was blowing hot and cold with Kuan Hee.

The two men bundled Kuan Hee into a small room at the side of the building. They forced him to kneel and kept their hold on his arms, which they pushed behind him.

"Now what have we got here," Wei Xin said, entering the room.

"You can speak English," Kuan Hee said.

"Of course. I can," Wei Xin said. "I spent many years in London as a student. So you are part of the group that's been destroying my labour of love."

"Labour of love? Bullshit!" Kuan Hee said. "You are bent on monopolising the world with your evil deeds."

"That's a laugh!" Wei Xin said. "We're merely orchestrating a change of leadership in our government. That's all we're doing—till you came into the picture. You idiot!" He leaned forward and slapped Kuan Hee in the face. "You destroyed five years of my work!"

"It's not your work," Kuan Hee screeched. "It's my dad's. You merely copied his ideas."

"Your dad?" Wei Xin said. "Now who exactly are you?" He stared up Kuan Hee's face.

"So you are Professor Wang's little boy, aren't you? You know, I've got your father's mind in here." He raised a finger and pointed it at his head. "Hahaha! I'm half your father!"

Kuan Hee spat in his face. "No. You're not! Not in million years. You're just a crook—a low-down dirty conniving crook. That's what you are."

Wei Xin wiped the saliva off his face with his hand. "You little brat! I'll teach you to destroy my best work of art."

He stretched out his hand and opened his palm like a lotus flower. The man next to him thrust a pistol into his palm.

"You will pay dearly for what you did," Wei Xin stammered. "You will die just like your father did."

He brought the pistol to Kuan Hee's eyes. "That's right. Keep staring. Stare at death in the face—your death." He let out a guffaw and squeezed the trigger.

Forcing his eyes shut, Kuan Hee screamed his lungs out and prepared to take the bullet. "Alex, destroy-fire-1."

The metallic-silver robot somersaulted into the room and landed in an upright position, legs apart and hands at its hips. The gears on its chest whirled rapidly and a laser at its epicentre unleashed a blinding beam that illuminated the small room. Its high-energy laser hit the man in the wheelchair, combusting him in seconds. Both Wei Xin and his wheelchair fused into a mass of white-hot substance.

Wei Xin's two minions were shell-shocked. Never before had they seen anything as deadly as this. They dropped Kuan Hee to the floor and scrambled for the door. Xander leapt into the room and stood guard at the door, legs apart and hands at his hips. It was the robots' programmed posture for attack situations.

Kuan Hee staggered to his feet. "Alex and Xander heel." He stumbled out of the room. In the open workspace of the building, Wei Xin's men had gathered. Some were brandishing pistols in their hands. It was six against one. Nope. It was six against three (one man and two thirty-centimetre-tall robots).

Suddenly shots rang out in the workspace. They weren't from Wei Xin's men. They came from the main entrance. In a split-second, a group of men in balaclavas had the entire workspace in their rifles' sights.

"It's the Brigadier's men! Hurray!" Kuan Hee shouted. Then he stopped in his tracks. The masked men were holding QBZ-95 assault rifles—the standard issue of the People's Liberation Army!

Alamak! I've gotten myself out of the pot into the frying pan.

Wei Xin's men dropped the weapons in their hands and squatted on the floor, with folded hands on their heads.

The masked men rounded their captives into a corner and stood guard over them.

Two men appeared at the front doorway. One was unmistakably familiar to Kuan Hee.

"Gosh! Mr Walmsley. It's you," Kuan Hee screeched.

"Ah. Kuan Hee. You are still in one piece. Thank goodness," Brigadier Walmsley said. He went up to Kuan Hee and patted him on the back. "Look at who's with me." He stood aside to let Lina face Kuan Hee.

Petite Lina threw herself into Kuan Hee's arms. She was gleeful with joy. She wasn't in tears! This had to be the first time she didn't cry in such a tense situation.

"Kuan Hee. Meet my counterpart from the Chinese intelligence," Brigadier Walmsley said. He ushered Kuan Hee in front of a tall brawny close-cropped man who had come in with him.

"Zhou Meng. This is the promising lad I've been talking to you about," Brigadier Walmsley said. "Professor Wang's son, Kuan Hee."

Zhou Meng proffered a hand and Kuan Hee shook it. The man had a strong grip.

"Thank you for bringing us to the human clones," Zhou Meng said. "We've been on their trail for some time. It's been difficult locating these clones. They've been hiding them in different countries."

Kuan Hee beamed. "Mr Walmsley, how did you find me here? Was it a coincidence?"

"Coincidence my foot, Kuan Hee," Brigadier Walmsley said. "It was you who brought us here."

Kuan Hee gave the Brigadier a look of surprise. "Have you been following me?"

"Perhaps, you didn't know, Kuan Hee. AleXander the robots and the drones broadcast their locations to the Polaris satellite 24/7," Brigadier Walmsley said. "That's how I know where you are every time all the time. So there's no need for me or my men to follow you."

The Brigadier paused for a breath. "What you see on the drone's remote screens, I see too. What AleXander the robots see, I also see. Every single frame and image is recorded in our servers."

"You mean—you have been privy to what we have been doing all along?" Kuan Hee exclaimed.

The Brigadier nodded.

"No wonder! You always arrive in time to save the situation," Kuan Hee said. "No wonder. You didn't need me to explain myself."

"Yes. Kuan Hee. Also no wonder why you are standing here safe and sound," Brigadier Walmsley said. "It's all thanks to your father."

"Dad? Why?" Kuan Hee asked.

But the Brigadier had no time to give him a reply.

"Kuan Hee. Zhou Meng and his men are on official business here. Let's leave them to do their work," Brigadier Walmsley said. "We've got to leave quickly. Don't want to attract attention from the neighbours."

The Brigadier waved to his counterpart and left the building with Kuan Hee and Lina in tow.

"Kuan Hee. Zhou Meng and I are doing our work without the knowledge of the Singapore government," Brigadier Walmsley said. He put a finger to his lips. "Shush!"

There were two vans parked in front of the main door. A tanned Caucasian was standing next to a car at the entrance to the compound.

"Follow me," Brigadier Walmsley said. He led Kuan Hee and Lina to the waiting car. "We're going to meet someone."

"Who is it?" But the Brigadier kept mum.

"I bet it's your mother. She's returned from Fort Bragg," Lina said.

Everyone piled into the car. Alex and Xander sat on the pair's laps.

"Let's move off," The Brigadier told his driver.

CHAPTER 36

The pair walked through the corridor on Level 2 of Tan Tock Seng Hospital with the Brigadier leading the way.

"We're going to visit Tim," Lina whispered.

"It's not a surprise after all," Kuan Hee said. "Perhaps, the Brigadier doesn't know we have been here before."

The Brigadier ushered the pair into Ward 5. There, lying on their beds were Tim and—Navin!

"Navin! You are safe!" Lina cried. She rushed to his bed to give him a hug.

"Not so tight, Lina," Navin said. "Kuan Hee will get jealous."

"Never you mind, Navin," Lina said. "He deserves it." She thought of telling their best pal about her fight with Kuan Hee over his rescue earlier today. Then she had second thoughts. In the end, she said nothing. *Let sleeping dogs lie.*

Kuan Hee and Navin gave each other a high five and the four adventurers cheered. They were all together again!

"How did you escape?" Kuan Hee asked.

Navin threw a glance at the Brigadier.

"You forgot what I told you, Kuan Hee," Brigadier Walmsley said.

Kuan Hee furrowed his brows. Then he spoke. "Oh. Yes. I understand now," Kuan Hee said. "It's Tizzy. The drone broadcast its location to the Polaris satellite."

"Of course. It is, Kuan Hee," Brigadier Walmsley said. "Otherwise, Navin would have ended up being dead meat." He chuckled. The adventurers roared with laughter.

"Mr Walmsley. Have you and the Chinese operative, Zhou Meng, been in touch over the human clones?" Kuan Hee asked.

"Well, it's a long story, Kuan Hee," Brigadier Walmsley said. "In a nutshell, the Chinese central government has been wise to the perpetrators' machinations. Zhou Meng is leading the central government's investigations into the plot to usurp power from the Chinese government."

The Brigadier paused to collect his thoughts. "This dastardly plan is the brainchild of Sun Zehao, a member of the Politburo Standing Committee—the highest decision making body in the Chinese government."

"All his underlings are being rounded up as I speak," Brigadier Walmsley said.

"The Chinese ambassador too?" Kuan Hee asked.

"Yes, he too," Brigadier Walmsley said. "The United States government is only lending the Chinese government a helping hand in this matter. We share the world stage. It is only right that we pool our resources."

The Brigadier surveyed his audience.

"The greatest achievement has been carried out by you guys," Brigadier Walmsley said. "Kuan Hee, Lina, Tim and Navin—you are all heroes. You discovered the evil plot. You went all out to destroy the human clones before they could do evil. You are all willing to place your lives at risk for justice."

He paused again. "That's highly commendable. Highly commendable indeed." All four adventurers blushed.

"Kuan Hee. Remember I gave you the diplomatic passport?" Brigadier Walmsley said. "I didn't do it for no rhyme or reason. It was with a specific purpose in mind."

Kuan Hee looked blankly at the Brigadier.

The Brigadier turned his gaze to Kuan Hee.

"Get ready for the next stage of your life, Kuan Hee," Brigadier Walmsley said. "You'll be using this passport regularly from now on."

"Huh?" Kuan Hee muttered.

"The sky is the limit," Brigadier Walmsley said. "Kuan Hee, fly as your father flew. The United States' Special Forces is behind you all the way."

"Hurray for Kuan Hee," Tim and Navin shouted.

"I'm happy for you, dear," Lina said.

CHAPTER 37

The Uber taxi pulled up at the gate of 79 Jalan Naung. Kuan Hee and Lina disembarked wearily. It had been a long day. The front door was open.

"Mum!" Kuan Hee shouted. The pair ran through the living room into the kitchen. The smell of food cooking on the stove led the way.

"Mum. You're back," Kuan Hee said. "Is that pork chops and baked potatoes with apple sauce?"

"Yes. It is, Kuan Hee—your favourite food," Mrs Wang said, smiling. Turning to Lina, she said, "I've cooked *meesuah* for you."

"*Wah!* It's got two hard-boiled eggs! Thanks Mum," Lina said. "It's my favourite."

"Have you guys been up to mischief again?" Mrs Wang said.

Kuan Hee flashed her a cheeky smile. "Aw. Mum. It's nothing like that. Honest. Lina and I were just watching 'Dawn Breaks' the movie at Cathay Multiplex."

The End

Some of the places mentioned in this book are real:

Atsari Hotel, Parapat
Brastagi, North Sumatra
Jalan Muara Takus, Medan
Jalan Naung
Hougang Avenue five
Lake Toba, North Sumatra
Parapat, North Sumatra
Sun Plaza, Medan

SINGLISH AND OTHER TERMS USED

Ah Ma: Hokkien for grandmother
alamak: expressing regret, shock or astonishment
Angmoh: Caucasian
Becak: Indonesian for pedicab
chia kantang: meaning Westernised
chop: official stamp/seal
huh: expressing disappointment
hor: added to the end of a sentence for emphasis
kakis: Malay for buddies
kampong: Malay for village
kopi oh kosong: Malay for black coffee, no sugar added
kretek: Indonesian clove cigarette
kway teow: flat rice noodles
lah: added to the end of a sentence for emphasis
mee rebus: Malay for a spicy yellow noodle dish
mee siam: Malay for a spicy rice vermicelli dish
meesuah: Hokkien for thin noodles made of wheat flour
mee soto: Malay for spicy noodle soup dish
tahan: Malay for bear/stand
wah: expressing shock or surprise
wah piang: expressing shock
wah seh: expressing shock

The author lives with his wife in an HDB flat in Hougang, an idyllic backwater in the North-East of Singapore. They have no children.

ABOUT THE AUTHOR

Raymond Han is a late baby boomer in Singapore. He has worked as a banker, an editor, and a teacher. After he left the banking sector, he found a second career teaching English Language to upper and lower secondary students in Victoria School, Montfort Secondary School, Greendale Secondary School and Hougang Secondary School.

Raymond also taught English at 'O' Level and General Paper to students in a private school for several years. He has a Specialist Diploma in Psychology (Counselling Psychology).